PAST DEAD

PAST DEAD

THE EXTRACTOR SERIES BOOK 2

MIKE RYAN

WWW.MIKERYANBOOKS.COM

1

Bridge was just outside the building, to the side of it, on the other side of a chain-link fence. There were some trees and bushes that he was hiding in. All he was waiting for now was Nicole to say she was ready. They were in Bolivia, working on the case of a kidnapped child being held for ransom because her father was a wealthy businessman. He traveled frequently and while he was away, the child was taken, her caretakers easily overmatched by the gunmen who stormed into their home.

The ransom was three million dollars, which the father might have been able to scrape together, though it would have taken some time. More time than they had. The kidnappers said if they didn't have the money within a week, that the child's head would be sent home in a box. It was then that the father made some calls, did some digging, and eventually came across

Bridge's name. It didn't take any convincing for Bridge to take the case. When a child was involved, he was in, no questions asked. He didn't even care if people had money to pay for his services when a child's life was at stake.

The father was supposed to make the drop with Nicole posing as his assistant. Bridge was coming in from behind, hoping to surprise everyone if things didn't go according to plan. If something went wrong, he'd be there to take care of it. And if everything went right, once the girl and father were to safety, he'd start taking the kidnappers out. He had no intention of just paying them and walking away, leaving them free to kidnap someone else's child. They were going down one way or the other. It was just a question of getting the little girl first.

They received a video call earlier that morning and saw that the six-year-old girl was still alive and looked unharmed. At least where it showed. There were no cuts or bruises on her face or arms that anyone could see. Mentally, everyone just hoped that this wouldn't scar her for the rest of her life. But that was a matter for another time. The first order of business was making sure they got her safe and sound and back home.

Bridge had been outside the facility, which used to be some small airport hangar. It'd actually been deserted for a number of years, which was evident by all the tall grass that was growing everywhere. Bridge had staked out the place all morning, as soon as they got word that was where the drop was supposed to be. He left Nicole with the father to make the arrangements and brief him on how everything was supposed to work.

For Bridge, all he wanted to do was see exactly how many people he was dealing with. So he was there and watching when he saw several jeeps of people driving onto the property. He watched twelve people get out, not including the girl, though she was led inside very quickly. There were twelve men and two women. They were all holding assault rifles, a few of them with ammunition belts thrown over their shoulders and across their chest before ending up by their hip. For a brief moment, Bridge thought about taking them by surprise right then and there, not waiting for a drop, not waiting for his partner, not waiting for anything. They wouldn't be expecting an attack right now. But as he rationally tried to think of all the implications, there were twelve of them, and there was a little girl inside that he couldn't see any longer, so he had no idea if they had someone with a gun on her or not. Plus, there was always the risk of a stray bullet hitting her. His cooler head prevailed, as much as he hated it, and he decided to wait for the others so they could follow through with their plan.

Once noon hit—the designated drop time—Nicole and the father came along. They stopped at the edge of the property, not yet in view of the hangar. It was a long drive up a windy dirt road from the main road they were coming off of. Nicole was driving and stopped on the grass next to the road, wanting to know what they were walking into.

"Luke, we're here."

Bridge looked at his watch. "Right on time."

"How's it looking up there?"

"They're all here. Armed to the teeth."

"How many?"

"Twelve."

"The girl?"

"She's inside. It's some abandoned airport hangar or something. It's a small place, but I can't see her right now. Looks like they got two guards out front, two out back, the rest are inside."

"The girl's there, though?"

"Yeah. I saw her walking in. She looked good. Didn't see any marks, seemed to walk fine. I think she's OK."

"You want us to come up now?"

"Yeah, go ahead. I'm not gonna make a move until you get here. Can't take chances with the girl inside. Once you have her, then I'll go in."

"OK, we're on our way." Nicole then looked over at her passenger, a father who looked as nervous as someone could be, which was understandable considering the circumstances. "You understand what's going to happen?"

The father nodded. "I think so."

Nicole felt it would be a good idea if she went over it again, just to kind of beat it into his mind so he didn't have to think out there and could just react. "OK, we're going to hand over the backpack, right? We don't give them anything until we see your daughter out in front of us."

"What if they resist?"

"If they want the money, they won't resist. Trust me, this isn't our first ransom exchange."

"What about the fact that there's not three million dollars in there?"

"They don't have time to count all of it now. There's too much going on. They wanna get out of here too. They'll open it, look through a couple stacks probably, might even dig around to make sure there's nothing funny going on. But the money at the bottom, if they look at it, they'll only see the money on the outside, not the fact that the rest are construction cutouts."

The man nodded, sweating profusely, not sure any of this was going to work. "You're sure?"

"Trust me. We'll get your daughter back safe and sound. I promise. Luke and I are both willing to die out there in order to get her back if we have to."

The man put his hand over his eyes, trying not to cry. "I just want her back. I don't understand why..."

Nicole put her hand on his shoulder. "I know this is hard. I don't have children, so I can't imagine what you're going through and won't pretend that I do. But believe me, we are going to get her back for you. I promise you that. You remember what to do?"

The father nodded, getting his emotions in check. "Yeah. Yeah, I think so."

"Let's just go over it one more time, OK?"

The man cleared his throat. "We, um, get out of the car. Walk about halfway to the building, then stop. If someone's out there, we put the bag down on the ground and wait for them to bring my daughter out. If they don't and wanna see the money first, we let them look in the bag. But they don't take it until we get her back."

"And after we have her?"

"You stand there while I hurry up and bring her back to the car and get her in. Then we get down on the floor and wait."

"No, there's been a change of plans on that one. What you're going to do is get in the driver's seat, turn the car on, and leave."

The man looked at her with confusion on his face. "But what about you?"

"Luke and I are going to stay there and clean up the mess."

"But you're outnumbered."

"We'll be fine. It's not the first time. And I'm sure it won't be the last."

"I can't just leave you behind. What if something happens?"

"Well, something's gonna happen," Nicole replied.

"And we want you and your daughter to be safe and far away when it does."

"But how will you get out?"

"Those guys brought jeeps with them. We can hot-wire one of them. Or better yet, just take the keys."

"Umm, what about the money?"

"We can send it back to you."

"No, no, no, that's the furthest thing from my mind. If you get the money back, I want you guys to keep it."

"Mr.—"

"No, please, I insist. I can afford to give it up. And it's a price worth paying to get my daughter back. So if we pull this off, please, take it. You'll have earned it."

Nicole smiled, appreciating his kindness, since they had never spoken of getting paid up to this point. "OK. If you insist."

"But please, do me one favor?"

"Sure."

"After this is over, assuming we all make it out, will you please call me and let me know you made it out as well?"

Nicole grinned and nodded again. "I will." She then sat back in her seat and looked at the open road. "You ready?"

"No. But let's go anyway."

Nicole began driving, taking about ten minutes to get to the hangar. It was a somewhat bumpy drive, not that it bothered either of them too much. They both had other things on their mind. Once she got to the building, she parked about a hundred feet away from it, not wanting to get too close for when the father and daughter had to escape. She didn't want them up close taking bullets.

"We're here," Nicole said.

"I see you," Bridge replied.

"Getting out now."

"Gonna start moving around back."

Nicole got out of the car, a rifle strapped to her back, the father doing the same. They walked around to the hood of the vehicle and stopped, waiting to be greeted by someone. It didn't take long. Not even five seconds later, a couple of people emerged from the hangar, weapons in hand. The two initial people were soon joined by three more. They started walking toward their guests, stopping about halfway between the two parties.

"You have the money?" the leader of the group asked.

Nicole looked down at it, the father still holding it in his hand. "It's right here."

"Let's take a look at it."

Nicole shook her head. "The girl first."

The man looked back at one of his underlings and nodded at him. The other man went inside the hangar, coming back out a few seconds later with the girl in front of him.

"Safe as we promised," the leader said. "Now the money."

Nicole looked at the father and nodded at him. He started walking toward the kidnappers, also going about halfway between the two sides. He and the leader were now only a couple feet away from each other. The father put the bag on the ground. The leader of the group bent down and unzipped the bag. Before he was able to look, Nicole wanted to make sure he understood the ground rules.

"Before you look at that, understand that if you try to take it before we have the girl, I'll kill you right where you stand."

The leader smiled, appreciating her candor. "Pretty big talk for a woman who's all alone out here."

Nicole shrugged. "Makes no difference to me. If you wanna get down and dirty, I'll play along."

"You realize I could kill you right where you stand without a second thought or much effort?"

"You'd go down first. And what makes you think there's not some type of explosive in that bag?" Nicole gave him a cocky type of smile, like she knew a big secret that he didn't. "Take everyone down with you when you take it back with you."

The leader looked down at the bag, suddenly apprehensive about looking inside. He did, though, and started going through it, though not very carefully.

"It's all there," the father said. "Three million. Just as you requested."

The leader picked the bag off the ground to get a feel for its weight. "Seems a little light."

"I promise you it's all there."

"I'll take your word for it." The leader then stood up, inches away from the father's face. "If it's not, we know where you live. And we'll be back for the rest."

"There's no need for that. I give you my word, it's all there."

The leader smiled. "Good. I'll trust you."

"You can pick up the bag, but you're not going anywhere until we get what we need," Nicole said.

The leader nodded at her, then looked back to his man. He waved at him to release the girl, who instantly went running over to her father. The man almost squeezed the life out of his daughter once she was in his arms. Then they quickly walked back to the car, getting inside as Nicole stood guard in front of the vehicle. The leader walked back to his men, bag in hand.

Once in the car, the father looked at Nicole, not feeling right about leaving her behind. But it was what she wanted, so he turned the engine on. Then, he drove away as fast as he could, leaving Nicole standing there in the dust from the wheels digging into the dirt.

"Looks like you got left behind," the leader said.

"Nope," Nicole replied. "It's just easier to kill you this way."

The leader started laughing, looking at a few of his men.

"Why don't you bring them all out?" Nicole asked. "That way I can see their faces before I kill them."

"Man, you got some balls on you, lady."

"Wish you had some. I mean, kidnapping a child is as low as it gets, isn't it?"

The rest of the kidnappers emerged from the warehouse, standing side by side in front of her.

"That's better," she said.

The leader thought something might be up, figuring there's no way one person, let alone a woman, would be standing there so confidently in front of all of them. He then thought about what she said about the bag and instantly threw it down, drawing a laugh from Nicole.

"Getting too heavy for you?"

The leader looked at one of his men and shoved him forward. "Check the bag." The man looked at his boss with hesitation, but he was shoved once again to move forward. He got down on his knees and started rifling through the contents. After he was finished, he looked up at his boss and shook his head. There was nothing there other than money.

"Looking for a job?" the leader asked Nicole. "Maybe I got room for you."

"I wouldn't be able to afford all the soap I would need to wash the stench of you guys off me."

The leader laughed again. "You are one funny lady, aren't you?"

"I figure it's better to be funny than dead. Which is what you're gonna be in a few minutes."

"Yeah? How are you gonna manage that? I don't see anyone else here with you."

Nicole briefly looked past the man, seeing Bridge running through the hangar to the front of it. "It's not what you can see. It's what you can't."

The man studied her face for a few seconds, trying to figure out the hidden meaning behind it. Then he realized she had help. She had to. He instantly spun around, looking behind them, some of his friends doing the same. As soon as they did, though, Bridge opened up, firing at them with his assault rifle, mowing them down with relative ease. Nicole quickly joined in the festivities, falling to the ground, shooting at her targets, then rolling over as a few bullets ripped into the dirt beside her, then firing some more. It was all over in a matter of seconds. Bridge took out half the gang before they even knew what was going on. The other half was taken out between the two of them with relative ease.

Once the bullets stopped flying and the dust flew into the air, Nicole got back to her feet, meeting Bridge as he walked past all the dead bodies. They briefly looked at each other, then checked everyone to make certain they were dead. They wanted to make sure there were no back shots taken on them once they turned away. Once they'd done that, they made their way to one of the jeeps.

"Sure took you long enough," Nicole said. "I wasn't sure how much longer I could keep them talking."

"You always do a good enough job of that."

"Really?"

"And how come you deviated from the plan?" Bridge asked.

"What do you mean?"

Bridge pointed to the road that led into the property. "Our clients are gone."

"Oh. I figured it was dangerous for them to stay here, even if they were hiding in the back of the car. Bullets can penetrate cars sometimes you know."

"Yes, I've heard."

"So I figured I'd let them leave, then we'd take care of everything when they left."

"And what if that made the kidnappers nervous, and they started firing upon seeing you left behind?"

Nicole shrugged. "Didn't occur to me."

Bridge smiled. "Didn't occur to you. That's what I love about you. So daring."

"Got the job done. Plus, you said they had jeeps here, so I knew we had transportation out when we finished."

They checked all the jeeps, finding one that still had the keys in the ignition. Before getting in, Nicole ran back toward the heap of bodies, grabbing the backpack of money before running back to her partner. Bridge turned the car on, then started driving back down the road as Nicole looked inside the bag.

"You know where they're at so we can return it?" Bridge asked.

"There's no need."

"What do you mean? Why not?"

"He told us to keep it."

"He did?"

"Yep. Said he was grateful for our help and that we earned whatever was inside."

"Isn't there a hundred thousand in that?"

"Sure is," Nicole answered.

"Wow. Very generous of him."

"Yep. Just gotta call him and let him know we made it out all right, and that he never has to worry about those clowns again."

"And then get out of here."

"I'd call this a good day, huh?"

Bridge smiled at her. "I'd say so. This was a slam-dunk win. Saved the girl, eliminated some bad guys... this is what we do this for."

2

Bridge woke up and looked at the ceiling like he had done so many times before, putting his hand on the shoulder of the woman next to him. He saw a sliver of light shine through the bedroom window, illuminating a portion of the bed. He looked at the time. Nine o'clock. This was usually about the time that Nicole would barge in and scare off whoever he had next to him. It wouldn't happen this time, though, since Nicole was the one sleeping in his bed. Nicole then woke up, rolled over, and kissed Bridge on the lips.

"Aren't you glad you stopped resisting?" Nicole asked, a wide smile on her face.

"I just hope we know what we're doing."

"Oh, stop worrying. We'll be fine. As long as you don't fool around anymore."

"No more fooling around?"

Nicole shook her head. "From now on, you're mine."

Bridge grunted. "I don't know if I can handle you all by myself."

Nicole playfully slapped him on the shoulder. "So what are you saying, you need help with me?"

Bridge looked perplexed and stared at the wall. "Wait, I don't think that came out right."

Nicole laughed. "I definitely don't think that came out right."

Bridge shivered, shaking his thoughts loose. "Just forget what I said."

"I usually do."

They lay in bed for another twenty minutes, kissing, hugging, and occasionally talking.

"I guess I should get dressed," Nicole said.

"Why?"

"I'm meeting with someone in an hour."

"Oh? Sounds mysterious."

"Might be our next job."

"Another job? Already?"

"People need our help out there."

"We just got back. What happened to breaks?"

"Terrible times don't take breaks for people."

They both got out of bed and got dressed at the same time. They quickly ate breakfast before Nicole had to go.

"When I get back, remind me to talk about our living arrangements."

"Living arrangements?" Bridge asked.

"Well, we can't live in this hotel all the time, can we?"

"Uh, why not?"

"We'll need something more suitable for the both of us."

"For the both of us?"

"If we're going to live together, we should have something a little more homey."

"Whoa, whoa, whoa, pump the brakes there, sweetheart. Who said anything about moving in together?"

"That's the next logical step, isn't it?"

Bridge's eyes darted around the room. "Umm, why is it?"

"Isn't that what happens when you're together?"

"It seems like we might have skipped a step or two, or, you know, ten. How about we just slow things down a little first, OK?"

"I just thought moving into a house together would be better for us."

"A house? Nic, you need to slow your roll. A lot of change at one time isn't good."

"For who?"

"For me! Let's just do this for a while, and if everything keeps going well, maybe in a year or two, then we'll talk about moving in together. Let's just keep the status quo for a while first, all right?"

Nicole rolled her eyes and sighed, but eventually agreed with him. Well, she didn't really agree, but she just decided not to argue. "Fine. I guess we can give it a little time. You really need to stop being so conservative, though. Open up your wings and fly a little. Explore."

"Last time I did that I crashed, so, nah, I'll stick with this." Nicole grunted and rolled her eyes again, then left. "Enjoy your meeting," Bridge said, though the door had already slammed shut. He then thought about her meeting again, thinking he should have asked about the location. "It better not be Mexico."

While he waited for Nicole to get back, Bridge passed the time by reading a couple magazines, then went on the computer and started reading the news. He liked to be informed of what was going on worldwide since his work often took him to all corners of the globe. He was still on his computer when Nicole finally returned about three hours later.

"Long meeting," Bridge said.

Nicole nodded but didn't say anything as she went into the kitchen and poured herself a glass of orange juice. She sat down at the kitchen table, across from him.

"So what's the deal?"

Nicole gave him one of those sorry types of expressions she sometimes gave when she was about to deliver bad news. She lifted one side of her face, her cheek rising up, half her lip curling, and one of her eyebrows changing shape. It was quite a sight. Bridge took his eyes off his computer and looked at her without turning his head. He knew what that look of hers meant. Usually something he didn't want to do.

"What is it?"

"Uh, it's about where we're going," Nicole softly answered.

Alarm bells immediately started going off in Bridge's mind. He could think of only one place that meant. There were a few places he wasn't fond of going, but only one where she would start the conversation this way.

"Don't tell me."

"I'm sorry."

"No," Bridge said, his shoulders slumping.

Nicole contorted her face again. "Uh…"

"No."

"I'm afraid so."

"No."

"Yes."

"No!"

Nicole nodded. "Yeah."

"Not again!"

"We gotta go where the jobs are."

Bridge pounded his fist on the table, though not really that hard. "Not again!"

"I'm sorry."

"Mexico?"

Nicole shrugged. "It's where we're needed."

"I'm taking a vacation."

"You can't."

"Why not?"

"I already took the job?"

Bridge made a few grumbling noises, tilted his head back, and looked up at the ceiling. "I hate this job."

"You love this job."

"I hate this job now."

"No, you don't."

Bridge glanced over at his girlfriend again, looking dejected and like he was about to fall out of his chair. "What part are we going to and for how long?"

Nicole started smiling, not able to keep up with the joke any longer. "I'm just kidding. We're not going to Mexico."

Bridge leaned back in his chair and put his hand over his heart. "Oh, thank god."

Nicole laughed. "Look at you. You're like... falling to pieces just over hearing the name of that country."

"I'm sorry, I can't help it."

"I mean, you're acting pathetic."

"Maybe so, but... hey, wait a minute, you know, that's really mean and cruel of you to tease me like that."

Nicole continued to laugh. "I know, but you should've seen your face. It was hysterical. You were like, oh no, not Mexico. You looked like you were about to start going into convulsions or something."

"I'm glad you had a good laugh at my expense."

"Me too!"

"Are you done now?"

"Eh, I guess so."

"You wanna tell me what our real assignment is? Or are you joking about that too?"

"No, we have one."

"Are you going to share at some point?"

"Well, since you asked nicely, I guess I can."

"Oh, gee, thanks."

"So as soon as you're ready, we're going to go see a man named Stephen Drewiskie."

"Stephen Drewiskie... sounds like a spy name. Or someone whose mother didn't like him very much."

"Or it could just be someone who needs our help."

"Yeah, that too."

"Anyway," Nicole continued. "Drewiskie wants us to track down some missing diamonds."

"Diamonds? Oh good." Bridge slapped his hands together, then rubbed them as if he were excited. "Haven't had a good diamond case in a long time."

"Are you finished?"

"No. I mean, who carries diamonds anymore? That's like, so 1950s."

"Can I go on?"

"Uh, yeah, go ahead."

"Thank you so much," Nicole said sarcastically.

"My pleasure."

"So Drewiskie is from California. He flew in specifically to hire us because he's heard of our reputation."

"And he's hiring us anyway?" Bridge asked with a laugh.

"You know what? If you're not gonna take this seriously, I'll just take the case myself."

"Hold on, hold on, slow your roll. Calm down. Go ahead and proceed."

"Anyway, Drewiskie is a pretty wealthy guy. His family owns some type of tech company."

"Obviously."

"Anyway, a few months ago, he was travelling, had the diamonds with him, and had them stolen."

"Months ago? He's just getting around to it now?"

"He apparently hired a couple other people first," Nicole answered. "They couldn't get the diamonds back for him. Then he heard about us. That's why he's here."

"Where are these mysterious diamonds?"

"Los Angeles."

Bridge scrunched his eyebrows together. "Los Angeles? Why is something about this seeming weird?"

"Well, he thinks he knows who has them."

"Then what are we needed for?"

"Well, here's the issue."

"I knew there had to be one."

"He thinks it's Los Angeles. It could also be in Brazil."

"So he doesn't know where they are?"

"The person he believes took them lives in both places," Nicole said.

"I feel like there's a bomb about to be dropped here any minute."

"The person has ties to organized crime in both countries."

"There it is," Bridge said. "I knew it was coming. And what's this guy's name?"

"Hector Machado."

"So it's likely that if we find Machado and the diamonds, it's likely going to be heavily guarded."

"More than likely."

"How exactly were these things stolen?"

"He says they were taken from his hotel room safe. He's got police reports, insurance statements, the whole bit."

"So you don't think this is some type of scam for a bigger purpose?" Bridge asked. "Because I really hate it when people use us as a prop for something else."

"No, I'm pretty sure this is legit. And he can afford to pay."

"What's he offering?"

"All expenses paid to Los Angeles, Brazil, or anyplace else the diamonds might be. He'll give us a check to cover costs."

"And after we get the diamonds back?"

"He'll give us an additional fifty thousand dollars."

Bridge whistles. "Whew, mighty hefty price tag. How much are these diamonds supposed to be worth?"

"About five million."

Bridge raised his eyebrows. "Five million?"

"That's what he says. And I looked at the insurance statements. That's what they say too."

"Wow. That's a heavy haul there."

"Yeah, and he's getting impatient about getting it back," Nicole said.

"This guy have ties to the underworld?"

"Not that I can find."

"So he's on the up-and-up?"

"As far as I know," Nicole said. "So what do you say? You wanna take it on?"

Bridge looked at her and gave a wide smile. "Let's go diamond hunting!"

3

Bridge and Nicole arrived at the hotel that Drewiskie was staying at. It was a five-star hotel that was only a few minutes' walk from Times Square. Bridge stood in front of the hotel looking up at it.

"Now this is a nice place."

Nicole crinkled her upper lip, not really sure how anyone could like a hotel as much as he did. She just didn't see the appeal. "Does it make you homesick?"

As they walked into the building, Bridge looked around at the finishings for the place. He seemed more interested in checking out the hotel than going to see their client. Nicole had gone over to the elevator and pressed the button, but quickly realized her other half wasn't next to her. He was still over by a wall, looking at some paintings.

"Seriously?" she said to herself. Nicole marched

over to the wall and grabbed Bridge by the arm. "Are you coming with me?"

"To where?"

Nicole sighed and slumped her shoulders. "Did you forget we're seeing a client here?"

"We are? Oh yeah, we are."

"Yeah. So would you like to accompany me so we can talk to him?"

"Yeah, I guess."

"Gee, thanks so much."

Bridge inspected the floors as he walked on them, thinking how nice they looked. They then got on the elevator and pushed the button for the twenty-second floor.

"I've never seen someone gush so much over a hotel," Nicole said.

"You have no appreciation for the finer things."

"It's a hotel."

"It's the quality and the craftsmanship."

"It's a hotel."

"You're not cultured," Bridge said with a laugh. "That's the problem."

"Oh, I'm not cultured?"

Bridge shrugged. "If the shoe fits."

"Oh, don't give me that if the shoe fits crap. Who's the one who was freaking out about going to a nightclub?"

"That's an entirely different issue."

"How?"

"Because that was business related, and I had very good reasons for not wanting to go."

"Which were?"

"You know very well what they were."

"I know they were stupid," Nicole said.

"They were not stupid. I just think at a certain point in time you should stop pimping yourself out with as little clothing as possible, dancing your brains out, OK?"

"So you're saying I was pimping myself out with as little on as possible?"

"Well, that one dress…"

"You said you liked that dress."

"I did. For me, yes. For others, no."

"Oh, so it's that whole jealousy thing again."

"It's got nothing to do with being jealous."

"Just admit it. You got so jealous when those other guys came over to the table."

"I'm admitting nothing," Bridge said.

The door opened, and they stepped off the elevator, though they continued their banter the entire way down the hall until they got to Drewiskie's room. Nicole knocked on the door while they kept talking. They didn't actually stop until the door flung open.

"Nice to see you again," Drewiskie said upon seeing Nicole.

"You as well."

Drewiskie looked Bridge over. "I assume this is the famous Extractor?"

"I don't know how famous I am," Bridge replied. "But I'm the one."

"Please, please, come on in."

Bridge looked Drewiskie over as well, though much more subtlety as he passed by and walked inside. He looked just as Bridge imagined he would. Kind of stuffy. Drewiskie looked like a guy who didn't ever get his hands dirty. Bridge's initial impression, considering the clothes his client wore, his shoes, how perfect his hands looked, not a single piece of dirt under the fingernails, was that Drewiskie always hired someone to do everything for him. He wasn't a man used to doing his own dirty work.

"Please, sit down," Drewiskie said, walking over to the table in the living room by the window.

Bridge sat down, looking out the window at the view. It was priceless. Nicole glanced over at him and saw that he was mesmerized with the view.

"Stop looking out the window," she whispered.

"Beautiful view you have," Bridge said.

Drewiskie also looked out. "Yes, it is. Every time I come to New York, I stay at this hotel. The amenities and service are outstanding."

"Nice place."

"Excuse him, he has a weird fascination with hotels," Nicole said. "He actually lives in one all the time."

Drewiskie smiled. "I completely understand."

"You do?"

Bridge pointed at him. "A man who gets it."

"Great," Nicole said, not really wanting to get into a conversation about hotels. She'd already heard enough about that in her time with Bridge. "Let's get down to business."

Bridge leaned forward and clasped his hands together. "Yes, Nicole said something about missing diamonds."

Drewiskie was already prepared with everything, having a folder of information at his side. He took out a picture of the diamonds and handed it to his guests.

"There they are," Drewiskie said. "Worth five million dollars."

"They're beautiful," Bridge replied.

"You can say that again," Nicole said.

They then looked at the insurance information, including the payout that Drewiskie was issued.

"As you can see, the claim has already been settled by the insurance company," Drewiskie said. "Nevertheless, I would rather have the diamonds back."

"And the money you've been paid?" Bridge asked.

"I've already been in touch with my insurance agent and told him that I'm actively trying to get the diamonds back. I've assured him that once I get them back, I'll return the money that I've received. And in turn, he has assured me that once the money's returned, then my premiums will go down once again as if no claim was ever issued."

Bridge smiled. "Nice to have friends in the right places."

"It's not the money that I want. I have plenty of it. I want my diamonds. They've been in my family for over fifty years, and I intend for them to be in our family for another fifty years. Somebody else should have them when we decide to get rid of them, and no one else. No one else has the right to take them."

Bridge nodded. "Well, I can certainly agree with you there." He looked out the window briefly before switching topics. "Nicole told me about this Hector Machado. How do you know he's the one who took them?"

"He's the only one who could. The only one who would have enough nerve."

"So you know him?"

"By name only mostly. He did come to me about six months ago asking to purchase the diamonds. I rejected his offering."

"Did you engage him at all?" Nicole asked.

"Not really. Like any good businessman would do, I listened, but I never seriously entertained selling them. Especially not at the price he offered."

"Which was what?"

"He offered only two million dollars."

"That's a hefty discount off the value," Bridge said.

"Indeed. I didn't even consider it. I thought it was more of a joke."

"Would you have considered it if it were a better offer?"

Drewiskie rubbed his chin for a second, thinking it over. "I seriously doubt it. I'm just not interested in selling them at the moment. Now, if he came to me with a ten or fifteen million dollar offer, I may have changed my tune. But as it was, well, you know the rest. I would have to be blown away with an offer to consider selling them."

"Do you know anything about this Machado?"

"I've been told he has connections with the underworld," Drewiskie answered. "That's about all I know of him."

"If we do this, and I'm able to get your diamonds back for you, he's probably going to know it's you."

"Let him. I'm not afraid of him. I'm a wealthy man, and I have friends in powerful places."

"Why us?" Bridge asked. "If you have powerful friends, you can use those resources to get them back, couldn't you?"

"Possibly. But I think that would take more time. And possibly use up favors I'd rather not repay anytime soon. Plus, I assume this will be dirty work. And you would probably be best suited for that."

"And yet I wasn't your first choice."

Drewiskie lifted his hands off the table, not really having a good excuse. "I chose cheaper and less well-known alternatives. That was obviously a mistake on my part. If there's one thing I've learned over the years… is if you want the best, you have to pay for the best. And that is why I've finally come to you. To rectify my poor decisions."

"That's all well and good, but now he's gonna know we're coming."

"How could he?"

"Maybe not me specifically," Bridge replied. "But if you've tried twice already, there's no reason to think you won't keep trying. He's going to have his guard up."

"I assume that's why you're getting paid fifty thousand dollars plus expenses. To do the work that nobody else can."

Bridge smiled, appreciating the bluntness. "Touché. So what kind of timeframe are we looking at here?"

"As long as it takes. Though I would prefer as quickly as possible."

"That's always my aim too."

"Is there anything else you would like to know?" Drewiskie asked.

"One more thing. Exactly how were they able to swipe the diamonds from you?"

"I'm still not sure myself," Drewiskie replied. "I was in Los Angeles, showing the diamonds at an event, a high-class event, thousands of people there, all with special invitations. I had the diamonds in a briefcase, showed them to various people, then sat down at the table and had dinner. By the time I got back home and opened the briefcase, the diamonds were missing."

"And you never looked at them again from the time you were at the table until you got home?"

"No."

"Probably did a switch at the table when you weren't looking or when you were talking to someone. They waited until you weren't paying attention and swapped it out with a different briefcase that looked like yours."

"That's what the previous people I hired said as well."

Bridge crossed his arms and looked out the window, obviously thinking about something.

"What is it?" Nicole asked.

"It's just... how often do you use that briefcase?"

"Hardly ever," Drewiskie answered. "There's really not much need to carry one that often."

"What are you thinking?" Nicole asked.

Bridge looked at her and took a deep breath, still trying to formulate his thoughts. "It's... if he doesn't use the briefcase often, then how would they know what it looked like? You're obviously not going to swap out a briefcase with any old thing. It would have to be an exact match."

"So someone would have to know that."

"Exactly."

"What are you getting at?" Drewiskie asked.

"What we're getting at is someone close to you probably set you up. Probably for a payoff of some kind."

"What? That's ridiculous. Nobody that's close to me would do something like that."

"I'm afraid there's no other explanation. If you carry that briefcase around with you all the time, then you could have been watched or followed; they would just get a duplicate. But if you're not carrying it around, how would they know which briefcase to get? It's a cinch they're not going to put down whatever comes along. You would know immediately that the briefcase was switched."

Drewiskie picked his head up, understanding what Bridge was saying.

"When was the last time you used it?"

"Before that event? Maybe three or four months before that. It's hard to say."

"Did you use it for the diamonds then too?"

"Uh, yes, as a matter of fact, I was in London at a jewelry show. I used it then as well."

Bridge looked at Nicole, knowing for sure that Machado had someone on the inside giving him information. That was the only way they would be able to do a swap like that.

"I'm gonna need a list of everyone who knows about those diamonds who's close to you," Bridge said. "Friends, family, co-workers, employers, acquaintances, maids, service people you've had out to your house, employees, and anyone else you can think of who knows about those diamonds."

"Surely you're not going to hound my friends, family, and people I know?"

"I'm not going to hound anyone. But if you want me to get your diamonds back, I'm gonna need to know who took them and why."

"I've already told you who took them. What good would anything else be?"

"Sure, I could go find Machado and get the diamonds back for you, but what would be the point? If he's got someone on the inside working for him, who knows you, he could just get the diamonds back six months from now. There is someone close to you who gave you up. I would think you would wanna know who that is."

Drewiskie looked uncomfortable agreeing to such a thought. He looked at both of his visitors briefly before finally coming around to Bridge's way of thinking.

"I'll get you a list."

"Thank you," Bridge said. "Now, I know Machado has them, but he had help. The first order of business is finding out who that is so they don't know I'm coming and warn Machado first."

"Fine, I agree with all that. I just don't want you hounding my friends and getting them upset."

"Mr. Drewiskie, how important are these diamonds to you?"

"Very important."

MIKE RYAN

"Then you need to let me work my way. I don't take interference from my clients. I'm very upfront with how I work. So if you're not comfortable with that, you need to tell me now so nobody gets too invested in this, and we can all walk away with no hard feelings. I'm gonna find your diamonds. And I'm gonna find out who set you up. But you need to let me do it my way. If I piss off a few people because I ask too many questions, that's just the way it is."

Drewiskie took a deep breath, still not liking that his friends and acquaintances might get grilled, but he nodded, agreeing to Bridge's terms.

"You're in charge," Drewiskie said, a phrase he wasn't used to saying very often.

"We'll go back to our office, work out some initial expenses, and get you a figure."

"Why don't I just cut you a check now for twenty thousand? Anything that's extra as far as expenses go can be applied to the fifty thousand bounty."

Bridge nodded. "That sounds fair. And I'll provide a weekly expense report to you so you know where the money's going."

"Hopefully I'll only get one or two of those. I would also like to be kept up to date every few days if possible."

"I should be able to manage that."

After finishing their conversation and getting the check, Bridge and Nicole left the hotel and walked through Central Park.

36

"Guess we should head to the bank first?" Nicole asked.

"Well, I don't think we need to rush. I have a feeling this is one check that won't bounce."

"So back to our office then, huh?"

Bridge smiled. "Sounded good. More professional."

"Oh, you mean you don't want everyone to know you live and conduct business out of a hotel room?"

"There is nothing wrong with hotels."

"Uh huh. At least this is a case that shouldn't take too long. We shouldn't have a problem tracking down and finding Machado."

"Yeah, finding him won't be the problem," Bridge said. "Getting in and finding the diamonds... that will be the problem."

4

Bridge and Nicole were on a plane to Los Angeles within two days of their meeting with Drewiskie. Once they got the list of names from him, that was all they needed to get started. When they got to L.A., they checked into a hotel, rented a car, and started their investigation right away. As Nicole drove to their first destination, Bridge read the list that their client had given them.

"Look at this list," Bridge said. "There must be two hundred names on it."

"I guess it comes under the old adage: be careful what you ask for, you may just get it."

"I didn't think it'd be this many."

"You know the lifestyles of the rich and famous. They always know lots of people."

"We can probably cross off family members. Or at least do them last."

"Why?"

"I doubt it was a family member."

"Why not?" Nicole asked. "You said you thought it was someone close."

"I didn't mean that close. Think about it; why would a family member do that? The diamonds are already in the family. Drewiskie isn't seriously considering selling them, and he planned to keep it within the family for another fifty years. So why bother taking them?"

"Maybe because it wasn't really theirs? This way, they keep it all to themselves."

"But we already know Machado has them."

"Unless Machado was hired by a family member who then sold it to them."

"But then you could never show them off yourself," Bridge said. "You couldn't flaunt them, show them to friends, nothing. You could never let anyone else know you have them, especially your family. Then what would be the point? These people, they get some kind of rush, a kick, out of people seeing the expensive things they have. They love people knowing how well off they are. They have to show off things like that. It goes against their nature to keep it secret."

"Yeah, I'll buy that."

"If it is an inside job, I think we're looking at someone who's disgruntled, or pissed off, and who got an extra payment for some inside information. And it has to be someone who's seen that briefcase."

"I'll have to try to get a look at the financial statements of everyone on this list," Nicole said. "See if someone has an unexpected high payment. Where are we going first, by the way?"

"Neighbors. See if they know of anything, seen any strangers hanging around, things like that. Then we'll go to Drewiskie's house. I talked to him this morning when you were getting ready. He gave us permission to go in his house, look around."

"How are we getting in?"

"He has a housekeeper who looks after the place when he's gone. He said he's gonna be in New York for another week. Said he'd let her know we were coming and to let us in."

"Sounds like we're set."

"Yeah. Let's do those things first, then head back to the hotel so you can start seeing what background info you can dig in on."

They first talked to Drewiskie's neighbors, but they didn't get much out of them. None of them seemed to know much of anything or had seen anything out of the ordinary.

"These people must stick their heads in the sand all day," Nicole said. "They don't know anything about anything."

"Some people just mind their own business."

Nicole shook her head, disagreeing. "No. On every street, there's always one busybody who knows what's going on with everybody else on that street. Always."

"Is this scientifically proven data that you're using?"

"It's my own proven data."

"That you've cultivated over the years from the apartment that you've been living in?" Bridge asked.

"Shut up."

They drove over to Drewiskie's house, which somehow didn't seem fitting enough to describe the house. It had five bedrooms, six bathrooms, an in-ground pool, a tennis court, a bowling lane in the basement, and a perfectly manicured lawn.

"Drewiskie said we could throw a ball down the lane in the basement if we wanted."

"What lane?" Nicole asked.

"He's got a bowling lane in the basement."

Nicole's eyes lit up. "No."

"Yep."

"A full-size bowling lane?"

"That's what he said. He said we could help ourselves if we wanted."

"Oh my... we have to check that out. I've never seen a bowling lane in someone's house before."

"Guess it's your lucky day then."

Once at the house, they knocked on the door and were let in by the housekeeper. They identified themselves, though it wasn't needed since the woman was already told to expect them.

"Mr. Drewiskie said you had full reign of the house, so help yourselves."

Bridge already started analyzing the woman, who

appeared to be in her fifties. She seemed pleasant, though not overly friendly.

"How long have you worked here?" Bridge asked.

"About ten years now," the woman replied.

"Drewiskie a good boss? Treat you well?"

"For the most part."

"Could you tell us where he keeps his briefcase?"

"His briefcase?"

"Yes. The one he kept his diamonds in."

"In his office."

"And where would that be?"

"Right down here," she said, leading them to the office on the first floor.

The housekeeper then let them be for a while as Bridge and Nicole started looking around the office. They immediately saw the briefcase, sitting on a shelf on one end of the room. Bridge went over to the briefcase and stood there for a minute, staring at the door.

"You trying to will someone into walking through that door?" Nicole asked.

"No. I'm trying to see whether this briefcase is visible to someone who walks by. Doesn't look like it."

"What difference would it make?"

"Well, if you can't see it from out there, then that means whoever copied it had to have access to this office, right?"

"That would make sense."

Bridge and Nicole walked out of the office to get the

housekeeper again. Once they found her, they brought her back to the office.

"Is this office usually locked?" Bridge asked.

"Yes," the housekeeper answered. "It is locked whenever Mr. Drewiskie is not home."

"But I noticed it wasn't locked today."

"Well, I've been going through the house, cleaning it."

"Oh, OK. So who else would have access to that office?"

"No one. Why?"

Bridge smiled. "Just trying to get things clear in my mind. So landscapers, pool cleaners, electricians, anybody like that wouldn't be able to go in?"

"Certainly not."

"Even if Mr. Drewiskie was home, would he conduct any business there with other people?"

"No, his office was off-limits to anyone except for business people in his company."

"And how often is that?"

"Not very often. He has an office in the city that he usually goes to. Most of the stuff he does here is just to look over various reports and business-like stuff, phone calls, things like that."

"And how often does he use that briefcase," Bridge said, pointing to it.

"Maybe a handful of times a year."

"So barely ever?"

"That's right."

"Could you write down a list of people who've had access to this office over the past year?"

"It'll be a small list."

Bridge smiled. "All the better. We're gonna keep looking around for a bit. If you could get us that list by the time we leave, I'd appreciate it."

"I'll get started on it now."

As the housekeeper left, Bridge and Nicole went around the office, looking at everything.

"What are you thinking?" Nicole asked.

Bridge looked at the door to make sure no one was there. "I'm thinking our housekeeper's as good a suspect as anyone at the moment."

"She's been here ten years. If she was unhappy, don't you think she'd have done something by now? Or that they would know something was fishy about her?"

"I don't know. I do know that ten years is a lot of time to build some hostility and resentment if you're not getting treated the way you think you should be."

Bridge and Nicole continued looking through the room, then eventually expanded their search to include the rest of the house. They didn't find anything particularly interesting or revealing until they got down to the basement.

"Would you look at this?" Nicole asked, staring at the bowling lane. "Look at this setup."

"Pretty nice."

"Now see... you can't get this at a hotel."

"I doubt there are very many places you could get it at."

"But if you own your own house, it's possible." They continued looking around the room. "Even have a little bar area over there, some seating, this is really nice."

"Yeah, it's all right," Bridge said.

"All right? All right? Are you crazy? This is fabulous."

"Yeah, I mean, I guess it has its appeal to some people."

"I know, it doesn't compare to your luxurious hotel."

"All I see is a lot of maintenance and upkeep here."

Nicole thought she knew the perfect comeback for him to appreciate the room. "But if you had a place like this, you would probably never have to go out again. You could just hang back in your own place, shoot some baskets, play some pool, drink at your own bar, play some ping pong, have a real elaborate setup. You wouldn't have to worry about mingling with people that you don't feel comfortable with."

Bridge kept looking around, slightly nodding, his mouth moving in a way that indicated he was agreeing with her line of thinking. "Yeah, possibly."

Nicole waved her hand at him, thinking he impossible to please. Sometimes she thought he disagreed with her on purpose just to get her aggravated, even if he really did agree with what she was saying.

"Well, I guess there's nothing else to see here," Bridge said. "Let's get moving."

Nicole excitedly went over to the bowling lane. "I just have to throw one ball to test it out."

"You've been bowling before."

"Yeah, but this feels different."

Bridge rolled his eyes and shook his head at how giddy she was at bowling a ball. She rolled a ball down the lane, knocking over most of the pins except for two.

"OK, you good now?"

"Oh, can't leave just yet," Nicole answered.

"Why?"

"I left a 3-10 split."

"You did what now?"

"The 3-10 split. I can't just leave it dangling like that. I gotta try to pick it up."

"Really?"

"Yes, really."

"How much longer is this gonna take? We're supposed to be on a job, you know, not bowling our brains out."

"Oh shush. Just one more ball."

"You said that the last time."

Nicole picked up another ball, rolling it down the lane, knocking over the last two remaining pins. She jumped in the air and pumped her fist in excitement.

"You do know you're not in a real game, right?"

"Oh, shut up," Nicole replied. "Stop being an old stick-in-the-mud."

"I'm just saying."

"You're such an old fart."

"Really? Lowering ourselves to juvenile insults, are we?"

"Not me, you old…" Nicole kept mumbling as she walked up the steps to the main floor, Bridge not really hearing the rest of what she had to say. Not that he really needed to know that it wasn't nice.

Once they got up to the main floor, they found the housekeeper again to let her know that they were leaving.

"Thanks for the help," Nicole said.

"My pleasure. Are you guys going after the missing diamonds too?"

"Well…"

"No, no," Bridge replied, cutting Nicole off before she answered and said something he didn't want her to. "Mr. Drewiskie just wanted us to check out his home and give some security suggestions. That's what we do. Security consultants."

"So you're not after the diamonds?"

"No, though Mr. Drewiskie told us about them. Of course that's what led him to hiring us. It seems he's getting a little paranoid about things since the diamonds were stolen. That's why we were asking about people who might be in the house and those things."

"Oh."

"Yeah, that's why we're here. To make sure nothing is ever taken from him again."

"You're really not after the diamonds."

"Nope, not our concern," Bridge said with a laugh. "Those little suckers are probably long gone by now. Besides, Mr. Drewiskie's already got his insurance payment for them, so he's not out any money."

"That's true."

"Well, we'll be seeing you. We might be back another time in the next few weeks to go over the house again and recommend some suggestions to Mr. Drewiskie about better security options."

Bridge and Nicole then left the house and walked back to the car.

"You really think she bought that?" Nicole asked. "About not looking for the diamonds?"

"I dunno. But there's no reason to let her know that we are. I got a feeling about her."

"What kind of feeling?"

"The kind that she knows more than she's letting on."

5

They'd been at the hotel for most of the day, Nicole getting into bank records for the people on their list. She was going down the list alphabetically. While she was doing that, Bridge put a call in to their friend, Eric Happ. He'd already read a good bit of information on Hector Machado, but he wanted to get everything available. About four hours after he called the FBI agent, Bridge finally got a call back.

"Hey, took ya long enough."

Happ laughed. "Believe it or not, Luke, I do have other priorities that don't involve answering your queries."

"Really? What else would be more important?"

"Oh, nothing much, you know, just the whole FBI thing."

"Listen, don't throw that FBI thing at me. Everyone knows the best government applicants join the CIA.

The FBI just gets the leftovers, and the ones who couldn't make the cut."

Happ continued laughing. "Oh really? Is that how it is?"

"So which one applies to you?"

"You know, if we weren't friends, I might just take you seriously and hang up now."

"Well, that's why we're friends. You know not to take me seriously."

"How did we become friends again?"

"It was that whole joint FBI-CIA Task Force that we were involved in," Bridge answered. "You remember?"

"I do."

"It was lucky you guys brought us on, or you would've never caught that guy."

"What? Talk about revisionist history! It was you guys who were having the problem. It wasn't until we came along that everything got figured out and we captured him."

"Umm, who was the one who put the cuffs on him?"

"That's got nothing to do with it!"

Bridge faked a cough. "Eric, who's the one who put the cuffs on him."

"You just happened to be there. Someone had to put the cuffs on him, and you were the closest one."

"I was the closest one because I was the only one who figured out where he was going to be."

"You are so delusional," Happ said.

"You still can't admit it, can you?"

"I can admit you have an overinflated ego as well as an overinflated recollection of your importance on that mission."

"That almost sounded like something intelligent. See? It has done you a lot of good hanging around with a CIA agent like myself over the years. I wasn't sure you'd ever get there myself, but maybe you've turned the corner."

Happ laughed again. While he knew that Bridge was kidding, it was starting to get his dander up a little. Instead of continuing with the banter, Happ was ready to end it and get on with his day. "What do you want, Luke? I assume it's not to kick sand in my face all day?"

"Indeed not. I had a question about Hector Machado. You know him?"

"Machado? Sounds vaguely familiar. Fill me in."

"Uh, splits his time between Los Angeles and Brazil from what I understand, involved with criminal organizations in both locations..."

"What are you looking at him for?"

"I was hired by a man named Stephen Drewiskie, rich guy, owns a family tech business or something. Anyway, Drewiskie has... or I guess I should say, had, diamonds that were valued at over five million dollars. He believes Machado stole them from him a few months ago."

"Five million? That's quite a haul."

"He filed police reports, insurance claims, all that

stuff. The police found no evidence of Machado being involved, and the insurance has paid out on the claim, but Drewiskie still wants his diamonds back."

"And that's where you come in."

"That's where I come in."

"Well, if the police say Machado's not involved, why does this guy say he is?"

"Machado approached him a few months, or maybe it was a few weeks, can't exactly remember now, but anyway, Machado offered him two million dollars for the diamonds, and my client refused the offer."

"So he thinks that Machado decided to steal them instead?"

"That's the thought."

"Gotta tell you... that's kind of flimsy evidence there."

"I didn't say it was strong, I'm just telling you what was told to me."

"I'm kind of surprised at you," Happ said.

"Me? Why?"

"Taking a case without much evidence beyond the ramblings and whims of a rich guy. You're basically just taking his word that Machado's got them."

"Uh, yeah? I've taken cases with less evidence than that."

"Yeah, yeah, I know. And how do they usually turn out?"

"With me wishing I hadn't taken them?"

"Just figured I'd leave you with some food for thought."

"Taken," Bridge said.

"Just because Machado's got a criminal record, and I can see on my computer right here that he has, and just because he's involved with some shady characters, and just because he was interested in the diamonds... doesn't mean he's the one that took them."

"You know how many times you just said the word just?"

"One more than you," Happ answered.

"Oh. Thought it was more than that."

"No. Just one."

"You sure?"

"Positive."

"Anyway, what are you gonna do if you go down to Brazil and break into this guy's house, look into his safe, find out the diamonds aren't there, then get captured, then find out he never took them to begin with, then get killed anyway because you pissed him off?" Happ asked.

"Why is it that every question you asked there was negative and assuming the worst?"

"For the record, that was only one question."

"Well, it was really like five questions in one. You cheated."

"But you still haven't answered it."

"Because I'm still thinking," Bridge said.

"You could get in a lot of trouble with this guy without even knowing whether he really took them."

"That's why I have Nicole with me. To save me when I need it."

"So you're gonna get her killed too?"

"No! She's not as reckless as I am," Bridge said. "She's supposed to be smarter. Don't tell her I said that, though. Don't wanna feed her ego."

"I heard that!" Nicole shouted from the other room.

"Thought I was talking softer than that."

"Nope. You weren't. And I have excellent hearing!"

"I'll make note of it," Bridge said.

"And what if this guy is leading you astray?" Happ asked, continuing his negative line of questions.

"Leading me where?"

"What if it's not about the diamonds? What if it's about something else?"

"Like what?"

"I dunno. I'm just throwing questions at you."

"Slow your jets there, Happster. Nicole has already completely vetted this guy. She swears he's on the up-and-up."

"What about that guy last..."

"Yeah, yeah, yeah," Bridge said, knowing he was going to bring up something unpleasant. "I know, there are instances when things have gone sideways for us. Things happen, mistakes happen, it's fine."

"I just wanna make sure you know what you're getting into."

"We do. Can you give us what you got on him?"

"I'll email you a file."

"I appreciate it."

"I'll send it over in a few minutes," Happ said. "Let me know if you need anything else."

"You know I will."

As Nicole continued going over financial records for some of their suspects, Bridge went over to his laptop, situated next to his girlfriend's on the kitchen table, waiting for Machado's file to light up his inbox.

"How you making out?"

"What does the look on my face say?" Nicole asked.

"Confusion, bewilderment, puzzled, baffled, muddled…"

"You know they all mean the same thing, right?"

Bridge smiled. "But also pretty."

"Awe." Nicole leaned over and kissed him. "Can we forget about work and keep doing this?"

"Not right now."

"You're such a party pooper."

"Work before play. And you never answered my question."

"Which one was that?"

"Have you found anything?"

"Not yet. Coming up goose eggs," Nicole said.

"Did you get to that housekeeper, what was her name?"

"Denise Ragland."

"That's right. You'd think I'd remember a name like Ragland. Rags. That'd be a good nickname."

"I'm sure that's what she's hoping for," Nicole said sarcastically. "A cool nickname."

"Yeah, anyway, did you get to her?"

"No, not yet. She's towards the bottom of the list. That whole R thing with her name. You know, I'm going alphabetically."

"Well, why don't you just skip around and go to the most likely suspects first?"

"I didn't realize she was on the most likely suspects list."

"Well, she is," Bridge said.

"Who else is on this list?"

"No one. Just her."

"Short list."

"The way I like them."

"What catapults her to the top in your mind?"

"I didn't like the way she answered some of those questions," Bridge replied.

"You know, what would you do if you didn't have me doing this stuff?"

"What do you mean?"

"I mean, if I wasn't an ex-CIA agent who capable of hacking into databases, bank accounts, and computers, how else would you get all this information?"

Bridge shrugged. "I don't know. I guess I would have to befriend another beautiful ex-CIA agent who can do the same thing." Bridge then gave her a sarcastic looking smile.

"You would too."

"Luckily, I don't have to. Because I have you." Bridge then kissed her on the cheek. "And you're all that I need."

Nicole smiled. "I like it when you talk like that."

"I'd like it if you found the information faster."

Nicole shook her head. "You really know how to ruin the mood."

"I haven't even started yet."

"If I find the information fast, will you give me another kiss?"

"If you can get it in the next five minutes, I will give you two more kisses."

"Three?"

"You drive a hard bargain. Three."

Bridge checked his email again, finally seeing Happ's name appear in the inbox. He quickly opened the email and downloaded the attachment. Bridge engrossed himself in what he was reading, so much so that he didn't hear Nicole calling his name a few minutes later. She finally tapped him hard on the shoulder to capture his attention.

"Are you listening to me?"

Bridge snapped his head to the side to look at her. "Of course."

"No, you're not. I've been calling your name."

He looked dumbfounded. "Yeah?"

"Don't pretend like you know."

"I was reading Machado's info that Happy sent over."

"Well, I'm done."

"You are?"

"Yeah," Nicole said, pointing to the screen of her laptop. "Ragland's info. Right there."

Bridge looked at the bottom corner of his computer screen to see the time. "It's been six minutes."

"Four minutes."

"Five and a half."

"Four."

"Are you sure?"

"Positive."

"I think you might be stretching it," Bridge said.

"It's six minutes now because it took you two minutes to figure out I was talking to you. But I was done in four."

"Oh."

"I'll take my kisses now."

"Would you like them now or later?"

"I'll take them now."

Bridge leaned over and kissed her. It wasn't such a bad deal, he thought. He then kissed her a couple more times. He even threw in an extra one.

"You gave me four, you know."

"I figured you deserved an extra one for doing such a good job."

"I like this game."

"I knew you would," Bridge said.

"Tell me why we've never done it before."

"Because we always kept a line between us before."

"Well, that was your fault," Nicole said.

"I might have been a little stupid."

"A little? Try a lot."

"OK. I might have been a lot stupid."

"Can I get that in writing?"

"No," Bridge said.

"Well, at least you know it."

They then started looking at Ragland's bank account, looking for any strange or large deposits made over the past two years. They went back much farther than they usually would have in case a payment was made well ahead of when the actual theft took place, which sometimes happened with such a large transaction. They first looked at any incoming payments over a thousand dollars, assuming she would have gotten paid a substantial amount for any help in getting the diamonds out of Drewiskie's possession. Once that turned up empty, they looked for any incoming transactions from the same source. With that revealing nothing, they lowered the payments to five hundred dollars, thinking they might have been trying to be sneaky by slipping under the radar with smaller payouts. But they turned up nothing with those parameters either.

"Hate to say it, but it looks like your instincts might be wrong on this one."

"You don't hate to say it," Bridge said.

"No, I don't. But the sentiment's still the same. I think you might be barking up the wrong tree."

"Dogs don't bark up the wrong tree. It's always the right tree. You just never see what they're barking at yet. But they know."

"Luke, just admit it. Your gut is wrong on this one."

Bridge continued looking at Ragland's financial statements, not yet ready to admit defeat. "Never."

"OK, well, you keep wasting your time with her then. I'm gonna do something more productive and continue on with my list."

"She's involved. I know it."

"There's no evidence to show that she is."

"I don't need evidence to believe it."

"What exactly do you need?"

Bridge pointed at his heart. "I just need my gut to point me in that direction."

"That's not your gut."

Bridge looked down at his chest. "Oh." He then pointed to his gut. "That's all I need."

"An expanding waistline?"

Bridge turned his head extremely slowly, looking at his girlfriend out of the corner of his eye, and giving her a nasty look. "My waistline is not expanding."

Nicole raised her eyebrows. "How long you gonna tell yourself that lie?"

"Are you calling me hefty?"

"No, not at all. I'm just saying you might not be as trim as you used to be."

"There is nothing wrong with my fitness level."

"I didn't say there was. I just said you might be carrying an extra five or ten pounds."

"You're calling me fat."

"I'm not calling you fat," Nicole said. "There's nothing wrong with the way you look. Some people are thin, some people are hefty, some people are in the middle. There's nothing wrong with being any of them. As long as you're OK with the way you look."

"Well, I'm sorry if we can't all look like Miss America."

"I don't look like Miss America. You're overexaggerating this entire conversation."

"Wow, you really know how to destroy someone's self-confidence, don't you? I mean, I always thought I was a somewhat attractive guy until you came along."

"You are attractive," Nicole said, kissing him on the cheek. "You don't think I'd go for just any old slob, do you?"

"Just the slightly overweight slob is what you're saying?"

Nicole rolled her eyes. "OK, this entire conversation has been taken way out of context. Can we be done with it now and get back to business?"

"What were we talking about?"

"Ragland?"

"Oh yeah. She's involved. I know it."

"You said that."

"And I'll keep saying it until I find the evidence," Bridge said.

"And if you don't find it?"

"Then I'll keep saying it."

Nicole was about to reply, but instead just shook her head. She decided to keep quiet and not keep feeding him items that would make him go off. He was already in one of those moods.

"OK, well, you keep doing what you're doing, and I'll do what I'm doing, and we'll see who's right."

"That'll be me," Bridge said.

"Braggart."

"I can't help it if I'm usually right."

"You just think you're usually right. You're not though."

"Well, I will be in this case. I guarantee it."

6

The examination into the bank accounts of everyone on their list turned up no abnormalities. They also continued their interview process, talking to everyone on the list as well, though that turned up just as many leads. Zero. Nobody knew anything, nobody saw anything, and nobody suspected anything or anyone. They had just gotten back to the car after interviewing their last suspect and began talking about what to do next.

"What now?" Nicole asked. "Everything's a dead end."

"I guess the only thing left to do now is visit Hector Machado."

"And do what? Talk? He's not gonna admit anything. You know that."

"Who said anything about talking?"

"What, you're gonna break into his house?"

"Well, break in, that sounds so crude when you say it like that," Bridge said.

"How would you like me to say it?"

"We're just going to take a look around the place."

"This can go bad in so many ways," Nicole mused.

"Yep."

"And which house are we breaking into? The one here or the one in Brazil?"

"Here first," Bridge answered. "If the diamonds aren't here, then Brazil."

"And what if they're not there either?"

"One step at a time. Let's just concentrate on this house first."

"I'm sure he's going to have some type of security," Nicole said.

"I'd be disappointed in him if he didn't."

"So what are you planning?" Nicole asked.

"I dunno yet. Let's put our heads together and think of something. I figure we got three options."

"Three?"

"We disguise ourselves so we can gain access inside, then take a look around."

"With a lot of people around, that could be a little dangerous," Nicole said.

"Danger is our middle name."

"Yours maybe. Not mine. Plus, them allowing some worker unlimited access to the entire house without anyone looking over our shoulder is pretty unlikely."

"I agree," Bridge said. "That leads to option two."

"Which is?"

"We sneak in at night, when everyone's sleeping, then tip-toe around the house until we find what we're looking for."

"You mean if we find what we're looking for."

"Right."

"And what's the third option?" Nicole asked.

"We sneak in during the daytime. We wait for the right opportunity, likely when Machado, or whoever is staying there at the time, leaves, then we go in."

"But we don't even know if Machado is there."

"That's why I said we have to stake it out first," Bridge said.

"You didn't say that."

"I didn't?"

"No."

"Oh. Well, we have to stake it out for a few days first. See who's actually there."

"You know, I really don't like any of those options," Nicole said.

"Do you have a better one?"

"No."

"Well then."

"I didn't say I wouldn't do it," Nicole added. "I just said I didn't really like them. Should I rent a helicopter?"

"No! And no bazookas either. We're in Los Angeles, not the battlefields of Omaha Beach in World War Two."

"So which option appeals to you the most?"

Bridge scratched his face as he thought about it, considering everything that could go wrong in any of the scenarios. And there was a lot that could. "I think we can scratch off number one."

"I agree."

"Unless we can get inside when whoever's in there is gone, save for maybe one or two."

"I think that's a pipe dream," Nicole said. "There ain't no way they're letting someone in without Machado's approval."

"Yeah, probably. That's why I discounted that one first."

"And the others?"

Bridge shrugged. "We could do either. Either way, we'll have to stake out his house for a few days to figure out the landscape."

They went straight to Machado's house from there, not wanting to waste any more time. They picked up some fast food on the way, figuring they would probably be there for a while. Once they got to the house, they parked down the street, giving them a good line of sight to the entrance. It was a big house, close to three thousand square feet, with four bedrooms and four bathrooms. It was a Spanish-style home, near the Melrose Arts District. There was a partial stone fence that was approximately five feet high that went around the property, along with a gate that went across the driveway.

"You just know the security system in that place is wired up like Fort Knox," Nicole said.

Bridge took a bite of his cheeseburger, then wiped his mouth. "Yeah, probably."

They sat there for an hour, not seeing any activity at all. Of course, it was tough to see over a stone wall sitting inside a car. But for now, they were content just seeing who was coming in and out of the property. That would give them a good indication of how many people were usually there. A few minutes later, they finally got their first hit of the day. A van pulled up to the gate. It wasn't hard to figure out what they were there for, though. The picture on the vehicle gave their business away. There were mops, brooms, and an illustrated picture of a smiling woman cleaning.

"Cleaning crew," Bridge said.

The driver in the van rolled the window down and leaned out, speaking into some sort of microphone system at the gate.

"Well, I guess we know someone's in there now," Nicole said.

Bridge nodded. "Yep."

"I was kind of hoping for the card system. Where they just swipe a card and the gate opens."

Bridge smiled. "No chance. Not with a guy like Machado. He wouldn't take the chance of a card falling into the wrong hands."

"And I'm willing to bet he's got guard dogs in there too."

"Oh, don't say it."

"Probably Dobermans, maybe Rottweilers, pit bulls..."

"I'd settle for poodles."

"Not likely."

"I'm still thinking about the last time I ran into dogs guarding a property."

"What were they again?" Nicole asked, trying to remember. "Shepherds?"

"It was a Belgian Malinois."

"Oh yeah. What's the difference between that and a German shepherd?"

"Well, one's a shepherd... and the other's a Malinois."

Nicole rolled her eyes. "Oh, thanks for clearing that up. Very helpful."

Bridge shrugged. "What do I look like, the dog whisperer? I don't know the technical differences. All I know is that dog nearly bit me in the privates."

"You're lucky you had on your extra thick pants that day."

"I can't even imagine the pain that would have...". Bridge then shivered as if he were trying to shake the thoughts loose. "I don't even wanna think about that."

"And that was just one dog. Imagine if this guy has two."

Bridge shook his head. "Then you can deal with them."

"That's fine. Dogs like me."

"What are you saying? Dogs don't like me?"

"Well, that one didn't."

"They probably had the dog all hyped up on coke and all. Did you see the foam that was shooting out of its mouth?"

Nicole laughed at the preposterousness of it all. "There was no foam shooting out of its mouth!"

"It was drooling like it needed a fix or something."

"I think what it needed a fix of was your pants."

"Oh, real funny for you to say. You weren't the one running from it."

"I helped you over the fence from the other side," Nicole said.

Their fond trip down memory lane was interrupted when they noticed the gate starting to open. Once it did, the van pulled in, the gate closing again once the truck was fully inside.

"We're gonna need pictures inside those walls," Bridge said, looking at Nicole.

"Oh, let me guess, that's my job?"

"I fully admit you're better at that than I am."

"So you want me to climb over those walls and find out if there are dogs there so you don't have to. That's it, isn't it? You want me to get bit in the rear instead of you?"

Bridge put his hand over his heart, pretending to be offended. "I am shocked, shocked, that you think I would intentionally put you in harm's way instead of me. Shocked. I'm... I'm hurt that you would feel that way."

Nicole looked up at the ceiling of the car and shook her head. "You might wanna change your shoes. Those ones aren't good for walking through all the crap you're spewing out right now."

"There's no crap being spewed out. If you were to get caught, you simply look less threatening than I do. Plus, you're a better flirter. So if you were to get caught, you could probably talk your way out of it in a way that I can't."

Nicole sighed, rolled her eyes, shook her head, and looked out the window for a few seconds, figuring out what she wanted to do. She knew he was technically right. She was better at getting out of these types of scouting missions than he was if they were ever caught. But she still liked to give him a hard time about it.

She looked around to see if there were any buildings in the area that would give her a higher and better vantage point, but it didn't look like it. There were a few buildings around that might have given a partial look, but that wasn't really that helpful, and if she had to break into someone else's house, that opened up a whole new can of worms, and then if she was found out there, that would put the entire neighborhood on alert, then it would make getting into Machado's place tougher.

Nicole took a deep sigh. She got out of the car and

went back to her trunk, opening it. Bridge got out and followed her back there.

"What are you doing?"

"What's it look like I'm doing?" Nicole asked. "Going to work."

"Where?"

"Here."

Nicole then reached into the trunk, where she had many gadgets and costumes, all of which would or could come in handy at any point. She then got out a green-colored neon vest and a yellow hard hat and put them on.

"Directing traffic are ya?" Bridge asked with a smirk.

Nicole looked at him and smiled sarcastically, then reached into the trunk again and pulled out a tool belt. "No, there's been a lot of homes in this area that have been experiencing brief blackouts. I'm going around, checking out houses in the neighborhood, making sure their electrical system is up to date and good to go so they don't experience any issues."

Bridge laughed. "You're never getting in with that one."

"Oh, you think not?"

"I guarantee not."

"I'm a cute, attractive woman with a tool belt and a hard hat. Who wouldn't let me in?"

"A similar cute, attractive woman that answers the door?"

"But if a man answers? Please. We all know I'll be in that house in under thirty seconds. We all know which body part men think with first."

"Their pinky finger?"

"Please, we all know it's usually smaller than that."

"Uh, not me, right?"

Nicole gave him a seductive smile. She pulled out a metallic clipboard, then closed the trunk of the car. "Can't talk now. Got a job to do."

7

Nicole walked up to the black steel gate, noticing a couple of security cameras looking down at her from a couple different directions. One was at the gate, mounted on top of the stone wall. Another was beyond the gate, located at the top of the driveway near the house. Both were pointed right at her. She saw a small red button sitting underneath some type of speaker system on a little black box in the middle of a concrete pole near the gate. She fiddled with her yellow hat before pressing the button.

"Yeah?" a man's voice crackled through the speaker. "What do you want?"

"Hi. My name's Nancy Douglas. I'm with the electric company."

"And?"

"Umm, well, we're here to check your wiring."

"Our wiring's fine. Nobody called for you."

"Uh, yes, I know. It's just that we've gotten reports from some of the people in this area of random power outages. So we're going door-to-door, making sure everyone's wiring is up to date."

"I haven't heard anything like that."

"I'm really surprised," Nicole said. "We've gotten reports from ten different homeowners just on this street in the past week. That's why I'm here, trying to do some preventive maintenance to make sure it doesn't happen again. I'm going from house to house. I've already noted wiring problems for three different residences."

There was no immediate response from the man, making Nicole think she may have been getting to him. Maybe he just needed a little extra push, she thought.

"If you can let me check your electrical panel, I promise it'll take no more than five minutes."

"Five minutes?" the man asked.

"Five minutes at the most, I promise."

The gates then opened, and Nicole walked through them. As she did, Bridge lost sight of her from the car. This was the part he didn't like. He hated not knowing what was going on with her. She was operating blind now. A million terrible things could happen to her in the next five minutes, and he wouldn't have had a clue. They could have placed some type of camera on her that Bridge could have monitored via a tablet or his phone, but with a residence like Machado's, they couldn't be sure they wouldn't have some type of a device that would have sniffed it out. Especially since she was cold-calling. They figured it was better this way, having Nicole act as unassuming and non-threatening as possible. But it didn't help Bridge's anxiety, knowing his partner, his friend, his girlfriend, was in there with no backup. He'd just have to wait it out. It helped knowing that Nicole could handle herself in a pinch, and even though she had no weapons on her, she still was well-versed in martial arts and could take out many a man. Hopefully she wouldn't have to use any of that knowledge.

As Nicole walked up the driveway, the gate closed behind her. She kept walking, finding a concrete pathway to the front door. As she got closer to it, the door opened up, with a man standing there and waiting for her. Nicole tried to take in as much of the outside as possible, without it looking obvious that she was casing the place and committing the scenery to memory. The man looked Nicole over as she approached, liking what he saw. She was certainly the most attractive electrical worker that he'd ever seen.

"You're here to check the wiring?"

"Sure am," Nicole replied with a smile. "Are you the owner? Mr... Machado?"

"No. Hector ain't here right now."

"Oh, well I should get permission from the owner

before doing any work or going inside. Will he be back soon?"

"Not for a couple weeks. He's out of town right now. I can authorize the work though."

"Oh, OK. Great. If you could just show me the electrical panel, I can get straight to work then."

"It's right this way."

"Oh, I'm sorry, before I come in, you don't have any dogs on the loose, do you? Not that I mind dogs, but sometimes when they see someone like me coming in, they start barking and things. I'd hate to get bit or anything."

"Don't worry about it, no dogs. Can't stand those furry things. They slobber all over you, poop all over the place, and leave hair everywhere."

Nicole smiled. "Oh, good."

The two of them walked through the house to get to the electrical panel, which was in the basement.

"Nice place you got here," Nicole said. "Well, Mr. Machado, I mean. Do you look after it while he's gone?"

"Yeah, usually." They walked down the steps to the basement, the man pointing to the electrical box. "There it is."

"Great, thank you." Nicole opened up the box and started looking at the wires. She wasn't an expert electrician or anything, but she knew the basics of wiring. After all, in her job, there were many a time when she had to cut power to a building. Sometimes it was to get

Bridge into a place, sometimes it was to help get him out. But she could speak intelligently about it without sounding like a complete idiot and blowing her cover.

"Must be nice to have the owner gone and have the place all to yourself, huh?" Nicole asked in a friendly manner.

"Yeah, it's not too bad."

Nicole fumbled around with a couple wires. "I'm gonna have to cut the power off for a minute, just so I can see how these wires react, OK? It'll be back up in a minute."

"Sure."

"You have people help look after the place? I noticed the maid truck out front."

"Yeah, they come in once a week. I don't do no cleaning or anything. Just make sure nobody breaks into the place or anything."

"Oh, that's a good idea. Mr. Machado's probably got valuables and stuff. I noticed some of the paintings as I walked in. Looks expensive."

"Yeah, he's got some expensive taste. He can afford it, though."

"I bet," Nicole said, putting the power back on. She flashed the man another smile and playfully touched his shoulder, making sure he didn't get suspicious of her. "Maybe one day you and I will have someone looking after our second and third homes, huh?"

"That'd be nice."

Nicole then laughed. "Oh, I didn't mean like, you

and me together." She then put her arm over her fore-head, pretending to be embarrassed. "I'm such an idiot. I'm so embarrassed. I'm always saying the wrong thing. Please don't take offense."

The man smiled at her. The thought of them being together was a pleasing thought. Even if it was only for a night. "Believe me, none taken. Do you, uh, like what you do?"

"Yeah, it's not too bad. Pays the bills, you know?"

"I'm sure it does."

"And you get to meet some interesting people sometimes. Some of them aren't so nice, but every once in a while, you get something interesting and crazy happening."

"Oh? Like what?"

Nicole got a naughty look on her face, pretending like she shouldn't say anything. "I don't know if I should say."

"C'mon, it's just between us. What's the craziest thing that's happened to you on this job?"

"Well, this actually has happened a couple of times." Nicole then looked around as if she didn't want anyone else to hear, not that there was anyone there. "A couple of times, I've met some guys, and we, uh... you know. Did it right then and there."

The man smiled. "Really?"

"Yeah, don't tell anyone. It's completely unprofes-sional, and I'd get fired immediately if anyone else knew."

"Is that right?"

The man moved in closer to her, putting his hands on her waist. Nicole let him do it, pretending like she was actually interested. The man leaned in with his face, looking for a kiss. Nicole turned her head away, letting him kiss her on the neck. She was actually repulsed and wanted to kick him in the nuts, but somehow was able to restrain herself. It was all for the job, she kept telling herself. After a minute of letting the slob put his hands all over her, she finally gently pushed herself away from him. She then put her hands on his face.

"I'd love to continue this, but I'm afraid I've got a few more houses to check."

"What's more important?" the man asked.

"I really have to get this done by a certain time."

"I'll make this worth your while."

The man started undoing his pants, something Nicole really didn't want to see. She quickly thought of a way to get out of there without having to do something else that was repulsive. She put her hand on the man's chest.

"I tell you what," Nicole said, talking in a sultry voice. "I have an even better idea."

"What's that?"

"Why don't I come back later, when, uh, you don't have any company upstairs? No maids, cleaning crews, friends, nothing like that. Just you and me. And I, uh, can wear something a little more appropriate for the occasion."

The man leaned in to kiss her, Nicole turning her head again, letting him kiss her cheek as they embraced. He kissed her neck again, and it took all the strength she had not to take him out right then and there.

"So what do you say?" she asked. "Should I come back later, wearing something a little more... revealing? I mean, if you're allowed and all. Maybe you can't have people over since it's not your house."

"I can have over whoever I want."

"So what do you say? I promise you I'll make it worth it."

The man smiled at her and nodded. "Definitely."

Nicole leaned in to him and whispered in his ear. "So should I wear anything underneath or no?"

The man couldn't contain his grin. He shook his head, giving her his answer. Nicole pushed off from him again, going back to the electrical panel.

"I should finish this."

The man looked down at his pants and tried to control the bulge he had developed. He then started tightening his pants again. While he was distracted, Nicole quickly opened her aluminum clipboard and took out a device and planted it inside the box. She then closed up the panel before the man looked up again and noticed what she was doing.

"All done?" the man asked.

Nicole gave him a satisfying smile. "Oh yes. All finished."

The two then walked back up the stairs, the man putting his hand on her rear. Upon feeling the man's slimy hands on her, Nicole really just wanted to give him a mule kick, sending him tumbling back down the steps, hopefully hitting his head and knocking him out. She somehow resisted the urge, though. They walked back through the house and went towards the front door. Before exiting, Nicole turned around.

"Nine o'clock tonight?"

The man nodded. "That'll work."

"Remember, just me and you," Nicole said, touching his chin with her index finger.

The man smiled, hardly able to wait. He then looked at her legs, thinking they filled out her jeans nicely. "Should I have the wine and music out?"

Nicole smiled. "Wine. No music. We won't have time to listen to that." She put her hand on his chest and rubbed it for a second, keeping up with the charade. "So, uh, what would you like to see me in tonight? A red dress? Or a black one?"

"Which one reveals more?"

"Oh, that'll be the black one. It's got those spaghetti straps, barely covers the girls." Nicole then gestured as to where the dress went. "And I have to constantly pull it down or else it starts riding up and giving me an extra breeze."

"Well, you won't have to worry about that for very long."

"Should I bring anything else with me?"

"Just you in that dress. I'll take care of the rest."

Nicole smiled at him seductively. "I'm sure you will." Nicole then walked outside and started going down the path to the driveway. She turned around, knowing the man was still staring at her. He was. "You won't forget I'm coming later, will you?"

"Oh, trust me, honey, I won't forget."

Nicole playfully waved at him, then went down the driveway. The gate opened up just as she reached it. She walked back to the car with a smile on her face. By her expression, Bridge assumed that it had gone well. She usually wasn't smiling if there were problems. Nicole didn't even bother to open up the trunk once she got to the car. She just plopped herself down in the front seat, took off her hard hat, and looked at her boyfriend.

After a few seconds of just staring at each other, Bridge couldn't wait anymore to hear what happened. "Well?"

Nicole couldn't hold back her smile anymore. "Told you it'd be a piece of cake."

"So what happened?"

"I've got a date tonight at nine o'clock."

"A date? I've been replaced already?"

Nicole rolled her eyes. "I told you. So many men

think with the wrong part of their body. Just show them a little interest and they're putty."

"So you have to go on a date with him?"

"Would you just shut up and listen to me?"

"Uh, yeah?"

"First, I think you owe me something for our bet," Nicole said.

"What bet?"

"You said I couldn't get in that house."

"It was longer than thirty seconds."

"Still, I got in. I think I deserve something for it."

Bridge looked at her in her outfit, thinking she looked kind of cute. "Maybe later you can check my power grid. Same outfit. Hard hat, tool belt... nothing underneath though."

Nicole smiled, then leaned over and kissed him on the lips. "That sounds like a deal."

"As pleasant a thought as that is though, can we get back to what's going on here?"

"OK, so Machado's not here..."

"What do you mean Machado's not here? So who the hell are you going on a date with?"

"Are you gonna let me finish?"

"Maybe."

"First, it's not a date. Second, Machado is out of town on business for a few weeks."

"Probably in Brazil."

"Maybe. Not sure on that."

"So about this date?"

Nicole's jaws tensed up. "It is not a date."

"You're the one who said it was a date."

"No, I didn't."

"Yes, you did."

"I did?"

Bridge nodded. "You did. I would hope that if I was being replaced, it would at least be the head man."

Nicole was about to lose her cool, but kept her composure. "You are not being replaced. Would you just let me tell you what happened?"

"OK."

"So I could see this guy was such a pushover. I just batted my eyelashes and he almost melted."

"So you..."

Nicole pointed her finger at him to stop him from interrupting. Seeing the stern look on her face, Bridge immediately shut up.

"So I flirted and flaunted, getting myself a date with him later tonight."

"See? You said date again."

"Luke..."

"I'll stop."

"Agreeing to see him later tonight was the only way I could guarantee that it would be just him inside that house."

"So he's the house sitter?"

"Basically."

"And what are we getting out of this?"

"The chance to snoop around the house."

"Is this before or after you sleep with him?"

Nicole's eyebrows raised, hardly believing what just came out of his mouth. "I can't believe you said that."

"Well, isn't that the plan?"

"The plan is to make him think that, not actually go through with it!"

"Oh," Bridge said, fully aware of what she was planning, at least so he thought. Somehow, she was even prettier when her face got red with anger.

"You're gonna owe me for that comment."

Bridge nodded his head to the side, not really minding giving her an IOU. Hers usually involved some type of sexual favor, so he knew it wouldn't be anything that he minded.

"Anyway, I'm gonna come back here at nine o'clock."

"The bewitching hour," Bridge said.

"Can you ever just..."

"Go ahead."

"So I'm gonna come here at nine o'clock. At five after nine, the power's gonna shut off."

"How'd you manage that?"

"While he was busy calming himself down thinking about what he's gonna get later, I was planting a device inside the electrical panel that's gonna go off exactly five minutes after nine."

Bridge nodded, impressed. "Good work."

"So you'll need to be ready. It should just be him in there. There are no dogs and no other guards, just him.

So the power should go out, also knocking out the gate, so you should be able to get in just fine."

"And our plans for Mr. Suave in there?"

"Knock him out."

"What if your device malfunctions and the power doesn't go out?"

"Then I guess we'll have to resort to alternative measures."

"As long as those alternatives don't mean..."

"Really, Luke? Really?"

"Hey, just saying."

"This is the quicker way anyway," Nicole said. "Did you really want to sit out here for days and weeks before figuring out how many people were in there?"

"Not really."

"So this way's faster."

"Just make sure you're not going too fast."

"What's that mean?"

"It means be careful," Bridge said. "I didn't see this guy, but chances are, if he's part of Machado's trusted circle, he can be dangerous."

"Don't worry. I've got him."

Nicole turned on the engine and started driving away.

"Where we going?" Bridge asked.

"I've got to get ready for my date, don't I?"

"Just don't get carried away."

"Would I do that?"

Bridge looked at her cynically. "Yeah, you would do that."

"Just sit back and relax. I'll do all the hard work."

"So who's taking this guy out, anyway? You or me?"

"Uh, I don't know. I guess whoever's closest to him."

"That'll definitely be you."

"I may not be dressed—I mean equipped for it."

"Really, Nic, really?"

8

Bridge was lying on the bed, watching TV, waiting for his girlfriend to come out of the bathroom. He was wondering how long it would take considering she'd been in there for over thirty minutes. Once Nicole came out, Bridge could hardly keep his eyes from jumping out of its sockets.

"Whoa. You look... amazing."

"Why thank you," Nicole replied.

"You look like... you're actually gonna sleep with him or something. I mean, why are you wearing something like that? Are you actually planning on..."

"Don't even go there, Luke. If you know what's good for you, don't even go there."

Bridge sat up on the bed, his feet touching the floor. He loved the way Nicole looked. She had a black dress on that maybe went to the middle of her thigh.

Maybe. And that might have been a bit generous. She had black high heels on to match the dress, which showed quite a bit of cleavage. If it were just the two of them, Bridge would have been ecstatic about the way she looked. But considering she was meeting another man, he wasn't too thrilled.

"But, I mean, look at you."

"What's the matter with how I look?"

"Nothing! That's the matter with it. You look hot, beautiful, amazing, and any other adjective I can throw at you. But that's the problem. You look like you're going on an actual, real date. You do realize this is just a cover, right?"

Nicole rolled her eyes and moved her jaw around, not really happy with his jealous behavior. "Listen, I can wear whatever I want."

"Of course you can. Who said you couldn't? I just think it's a little inappropriate."

"Luke, he's expecting me to come all dressed up like this, assuming he's gonna get a little action. Now, if I show up there, all covered up looking like a nun, I highly doubt he's gonna get all warm and fuzzy, do you?"

"I could live with that."

"If I go there in jeans and a dirty T-shirt, don't you think he's gonna get a little suspicious?"

"I have an idea."

"That makes an even one for this month."

Bridge pretended to laugh. "Ha. Very funny."

"It wasn't meant to be."

"Yeah, anyway, why don't we just wait until 9:05 p.m., then the lights will go off, then we go in. There, problem solved." Bridge then wiped his hands like he had solved a mystery.

"Umm, the problem with that is that we won't know where he is either. He's not just gonna stand around near the gate waiting for one of us to clobber him over the head."

"I'll put on my night-vision goggles."

Nicole sighed and shook her head. "Why do you have to make things so difficult? We had a perfectly good plan, made by me, and now you're screwing everything up."

"I just... I just don't like other men seeing you... like that."

Nicole walked over to him, a grin on her face. He was jealous, but she kind of liked it. It wasn't an overbearing type of jealousy, he wasn't controlling or anything like that, but she liked the fact that he didn't want anyone else looking at her. As long as it never manifested itself into a boiling type of rage like some women experienced with jealous partners, she was fine with it. But she knew she would never have to worry about Bridge displaying that type of rage. It just wasn't him. Nicole sat down on Bridge's lap, putting her arms around his neck. She then leaned in and kissed him a few times.

"I promise you, nothing's going to happen."

Bridge managed a smile. "I know."

Nicole lifted up his chin with her finger, kissing him again. "You're the only one I will ever let take this dress off me."

"I like the sound of that."

"And, uh, maybe after we're done... maybe we can come back here and... do stuff."

"What kind of stuff did you have in mind?"

Nicole kissed him again. "I think you know the answer to that."

Bridge couldn't stop smiling now, liking what he had in store later. "I could definitely go for that."

"I thought you could."

Bridge then looked at the time. "We still got some time before we need to leave. Maybe we could have a little before-party?"

Nicole looked at the time too, seeing that they had over an hour to go before nine o'clock. And it only took about twenty-five minutes to get to Machado's place. She gave Bridge a seductive glance and playfully pushed him down on the bed before sitting on top of his lower half. "Now you're talking my language."

Bridge and Nicole arrived at the Machado residence about ten minutes before nine. She was hoping to get there a little earlier, but considering the activities they were engaged in before leaving the hotel, she had to get herself ready all over again. Still, they made it in time, which was all that really mattered.

"How do I look?"

Bridge closed his eyes and shook his head. "You already know how you look."

"Well, I just wanna look presentable."

Bridge looked down at her well-tanned legs, of which there was much to be seen of in that dress. "You know, I think sometimes you just like hearing how good you look. It's not even about making me jealous, or looking presentable, you just want to hear me say how good you look."

Nicole painted on a smile, not confirming or denying his assumption. "A question for another day."

"You say I avoid questions. I've been noticing you've been doing quite a bit of that lately too."

"Well, I learned from the master."

Nicole then leaned over and kissed him, making sure he had a good view of her cleavage as well.

"Just make sure he's only looking at the goods and not touching," Bridge said.

Nicole kissed him again. "I promise."

"And not looking too long either. No window shopping."

Nicole ran her fingers over his hair, not that there was much with his military-style haircut. But she did what she could with it. "You know you're cute when you're jealous."

"I'm not jealous."

"OK. When you're concerned."

"Just make sure you're not in there too long."

"You just make sure you're ready by 9:05 p.m.," Nicole said. "I can only keep him at arm's length for so long."

"Now who's kidding who? We both know you could take out that guy long before I get in there. You just wanna make me work for it."

Nicole smiled and shrugged, sounding happy about it. "Maybe." Nicole looked at the time on the dashboard, seeing it was two minutes to nine. "Whoops, gotta go!" She got out of the car and closed the door, leaning back in through the open window. "Remember... don't be late."

"Wouldn't dream of it."

Bridge watched Nicole's every step on the way to the front gate, enjoying how her body moved in that dress, along with the parts that were exposed outside of it. He kept looking at the time, wishing that it would speed up, not that they had long to go, anyway. When she got to the gate, Nicole pressed the red button.

"Yes?"

Nicole moved closer to the speaker. "Hi. It's Nancy. You remember me from earlier? The electrician?"

"Oh, I remember."

"Did you still want me to come in? I dressed for the occasion."

"I've been waiting all day for this. Hold on."

The gate then opened, with Nicole slipping through. The gate quickly closed behind her. Bridge watched from his car, wishing he could've slipped inside with her, but knowing there were cameras there, he wouldn't have gotten in unseen. He just had to let the process play out. As Nicole walked up the driveway, then on the concrete path to the door, she thought about how much she hated doing this. She didn't like dressing up this way, parading her body around like she was some sex maniac who would sleep with whatever man was closest to her. She played it off like she didn't mind, mostly because she knew how much it got to her now boyfriend, and she liked getting him riled up, but she wouldn't have done it if she didn't think it was necessary. She really didn't like other men looking at her like some sex object, unless it was Bridge, of course. He could look at her all day like that if he wanted to.

But at least it was for only five minutes this time. As long as the device cooperated and went off on time. Every now and then there would be a hiccup with one of those things where it didn't do what it was supposed to, or it would go off twenty minutes after it should have, or once in a while, it wouldn't go off at all. She hoped this was one of those times when it went off without a hitch. She was counting on it. Because if it didn't go off on time, there was no telling what she would do to this guy if he tried putting his hands on her again.

As Nicole got to the door, it opened, revealing the same man she'd talked to earlier. He was almost foaming at the mouth as he saw her approach. The smile on his face indicated he was very much pleased with what he was seeing. Nicole already felt dirty, seeing his eyes look at every part of her body, though they didn't seem to focus on her face very much. She supposed that was the look she was going for. To get him distracted in whatever way possible. This seemed to do the trick.

"You look... mmm, mmm, mmm. I could just taste you right now."

Nicole wanted to throw up in her mouth right then and there, but she was able to resist the temptation. "Well, that's what I was hoping for."

The man stepped aside, letting the beautiful woman inside. He looked at the back of her as she walked in, paying special attention to her backside, thinking he must have been extremely lucky to be able to have a night like this with a woman like that.

"You did send everyone else away, right?" Nicole asked, turning around so he could get a good look. "I'd hate to think I dressed like this for nothing."

"Don't worry. It's just me and you."

The man closed the door and walked over to her, trying to put his hands around her waist and move in for a kiss. She put a quick stop to that.

"Not so fast. You're gonna have to work for it a bit

first. Don't you have some wine or something? I get a lot more... playful once I have some alcohol in me."

The man smiled, hardly able to contain himself with the action he believed he was soon going to get. "Yeah, I got something."

He walked into the kitchen, pouring them both a glass of wine. Nicole had wandered into the living room, sitting down on the couch in front of the fireplace. She took a look at the time to figure out how much longer she had to stall. Only a couple minutes to go. The man came back in with the two glasses, giving her one as he sat down next to her.

"So do you do this often when the boss is away?"

The man moved in closer to her. "Not often enough."

The two of them clanged their glasses together before taking a sip of their red wine. The man set his glass on the floor, then put his hand on Nicole's knee, and started making his way up her thigh. Nicole plastered on a smile but wasn't about to let him get farther than that. She grabbed his hand and took it off her leg.

"What's the matter?"

"Nothing," Nicole said pleasantly. "I made you a promise though, didn't I?"

"You did?"

"I promised nothing would be on underneath."

The man smiled. "That's right."

"I'm always a girl of my word. Do you, uh, have a bathroom where I can... get more comfortable?"

The man looked over to the hallway where the bathroom was located. He leaned back on the couch. "Over there."

Nicole seductively looked at him as she got him. "Don't go anywhere."

"Believe me, I won't."

"I'll be right back. And I promise things will be... much smoother."

The man kept the smile on his face as he watched her walk away, admiring her athletic looking legs. Anticipating the moment when she got back, he took off his belt and unzipped his pants.

Safely in the bathroom, Nicole looked at her watch. She didn't want to be in there when the power went off and possibly lose sight of her target, so she came out with about thirty seconds to go. By this time, Bridge had gotten out of the car and was walking along the stone fence. He made sure he didn't walk in front of the gate or in front of any cameras that may have been watching. Once Nicole came out of the bathroom, she instantly saw her new friend sitting on the couch, his hands on his pants, anxiously awaiting her arrival. She noticed he had fiddled around with his pants in her absence.

"I see you've made good use of your time while I was gone."

"I don't like to wait."

"You're not much for foreplay, are you?"

"Not when I have someone who looks like you right in front of me."

Nicole smiled uncomfortably. "I bet you're a hit with all the ladies."

Nicole had been counting down the time since she had left the bathroom. A few more seconds and the lights should have been going out. Once she got down to the last few seconds, she waited for the room to go dark. Her eyes stayed wide open, hardly blinking at all as they stayed on. The look wasn't lost on the man in front of her.

"What's wrong?"

Nicole quickly had to regain her composure, even though she was cursing under her breath about the functional ability of the device she'd planted earlier.

"Nothing. Nothing at all. I was just thinking about..." She looked down at the bulge in his pants to ease his mind. "About some of the things I was planning on doing."

"Oh yeah? Like what? Show me."

Nicole sighed, figuring she was just going to have to do things the hard way. She had no intention of doing anything other than what she'd originally intended. She moved in a little closer to the man. She was just about to use a few of the moves that she had been practicing with Bridge, when suddenly the lights went out. She closed her eyes and took a deep breath.

"Finally," she muttered. "Took you long enough."

"Hey, what's happening?"

"Just relax, it's probably those blackouts that I had been telling you about."

"I thought you fixed that."

"Well… it's OK though. We were gonna turn the lights out anyway, weren't we?"

"Yeah, guess we were."

"It's fine. It's better that you don't see this coming," Nicole said.

"What's that?"

Nicole moved in a little closer, then quickly spun around, slipping off her high-heeled shoe in the process. As she spun back around, she lifted her leg up, delivering a powerful kick that connected square to the man's face, the heel of her foot nailing him right in the bridge of the nose. The man slumped over onto the couch, though he wasn't yet incapacitated. A little groggy, and in some pain, he reached up to his nose, fearing it was broken. There was some blood dripping down from it, and it was slightly out of place from its previous position. He got back to his feet, ready to take the woman on.

"What'd you do that for?!"

"I heard you liked it rough," Nicole replied.

She wasn't about to let him get in a shot. She instantly delivered another kick, her leg reaching up to the side of the man's head, hitting him with another powerful shot. This one knocked him over again. He fell back onto the couch once more, though this time, he wasn't getting back up. He was knocked out cold.

Satisfied with her work, she went over to him and checked to see if he was still breathing. He might have been a pig, but she didn't want to kill him. He hadn't done anything to warrant that. At least not that she knew of.

"That's for touching my ass earlier. Bastard."

9

_____

As soon as he saw the lights turn out, Bridge pushed on the gate, opening it with ease since it was no longer connected to the power. He ran up the driveway, then over to the door. He anxiously opened it, hoping to see Nicole as soon as he went in. It was dark, though, and he couldn't immediately see much.

"Nic?"

He saw the outline of someone coming closer to him. He readied himself for a fight in case it wasn't his girlfriend. Thankfully, as she got near, he could see the nice shape of her outline. She gradually became clearer as she came closer to the door, the light of the moon illuminating her shapely frame. Nicole came up to him and planted a kiss on his lips.

"Told you it would work."

Bridge looked at his watch. "It's 9:07. A little late."

"So there was a small issue. It worked. That's the bottom line."

"And our guy?"

Nicole smiled. "Sleeping like a baby."

"Have any trouble with him?"

"Two shots and he was out."

"How long do we have?"

"Till he wakes up?"

"Till the power comes back on."

"Oh. That should come back on in another minute or two," Nicole replied. "It only cuts the power for a few minutes."

"Good. I hate looking for things in the dark." Bridge put his hand on his girlfriend's back as they walked back inside. "Get a chance to look for anything yet?"

"No, I was waiting until you got here."

They stood in the living room by the couch where the man was knocked out. "I wonder how long he'll be sleeping for?"

"I hit him pretty hard. I think we'll be long gone by the time he wakes up again."

They waited another minute, then the power came back on. They both looked up at the lights as the room lit up. Then, they heard something. They definitely weren't alone.

"What was that?" Bridge asked, somewhat terrified in knowing something else was there.

"I don't know. That jerk said we were alone. He lied to me."

"Imagine that. He wasn't trustworthy."

They continued listening, the sound getting louder and coming closer.

"Sounds like someone's growling," Bridge said. His eyes almost popped out of his head when he heard a bark. It sounded like a large animal. "That's a dog!"

"Uh, yeah, yeah, sure sounds like it."

They didn't have to wait much longer, as the body of the animal suddenly ran out from the hallway and into the room.

"You said there were no dogs!"

"That's what he told me!" Nicole replied.

Bridge immediately started running, knowing the animal was coming for him. "Save yourself!" He ran into the kitchen, the animal running right past Nicole like she wasn't even there.

"Uh..." Nicole shrugged, not knowing what else to do.

She followed the dog into the kitchen, where she saw Bridge climb on top of the kitchen counter. The dog jumped up and put his paws on top of the counter, barking at the strange man. Nicole stood in the frame of the door, her arms folded across her chest, just looking at them and shaking her head.

"Look at you."

"Look at me?!" Bridge said, being careful to not

allow any body parts to get within range of the dog's mouth. "Look at you!"

The dog looked back at Nicole, though he didn't seem very interested in her.

"Why do you get to just stand there and not be in fear of your life?"

Nicole angled her head as she thought. "I guess you look more threatening than I do."

"He's probably a boy dog."

"What's that got to do with it."

"He probably saw you in that dress and his boy urges kicked into gear, then he just went after me instead."

Nicole rolled her eyes, thinking it sounded ridiculous. "It's amazing the things you think of."

"What kind of dog is this?"

Nicole looked the dog over, though it was pretty easy to ascertain what it was with its distinctive look. "Looks like a Doberman."

"Well, since you seem to have gotten a free pass here, you wanna try helping me and get him away?"

Nicole smiled. "I dunno. Looks kind of funny and all."

"It's not gonna be that funny if that guy wakes up while we're in here."

"Yeah, I guess so."

"Gee, thanks, as long as you have nothing better to do."

Nicole laughed. "The positions you get yourself into sometimes."

"Hey, you told me there were no dogs here."

"All I can do is repeat the information I'm told."

"Well, apparently your good looks aren't enough to not get bad intel."

Nicole shrugged. "Happens to everybody."

"Think you can help me out now?"

Nicole laughed to herself. "Sure. I can help you out… again. One more time… extracting The Extractor."

"Now's not the time for the play on words, Nic. Now's really not the time."

"OK, OK." Nicole got down on one knee. "C'mere boy. Come here."

"You sure it's a boy?"

Nicole leaned over, looking at the dog's underbelly. "Uh, yeah, pretty sure." She kept calling for him, though he seemed more interested in Bridge at the moment. "Come on, boy."

After a few more seconds, the dog finally put all his paws back down on the floor. He looked back at Nicole again, then lazily walked over to her. He put his head on her leg once he got to her. Bridge started to get off the counter, but the dog looked back at him and started growling. Bridge quickly resumed his position on the counter.

"OK, now that you and Cujo have made friends there, you think you can get him out of here?"

Nicole looked at him like she was offended. "He is not a bad dog. He is a good dog. Aren't you?" She put her face in front of the dog's, letting him lick it as she rubbed behind his ears.

"Well, at least you got dressed up for somebody who's giving you kisses tonight."

"Shut up."

"Umm, if you and the dog are done loving it up, you think you can get him out of here at some point? Unless you want me to just..."

"No! You will not hurt him."

"I was just saying."

"Come here, buddy."

Nicole got up and grabbed the dog by the collar, leading him through the house. She wanted him to be safe and eventually led him to the back door, putting him in the yard, which was fenced. She knew the front gate was open and didn't want the dog to get loose through there, but remembered seeing a chain-link fence to separate the back and front yards. Part of her thought that maybe she should just free the dog, figuring he shouldn't be with owners the likes of Machado. But upon looking the dog over, it appeared he was being taken care of. He was well-fed, no marks or scars on him like he was beaten, he didn't appear fearful of humans or of being touched, and therefore no reason to set him loose.

Nicole came back through the house after putting

the dog in the yard, seeing Bridge still atop the counter in the kitchen.

"You just gonna sit up there all night?"

"Well, you never know," Bridge replied. "I wanted to make sure that beast was outside."

"He is not a beast. He was a friendly, loving dog."

"Says the person who wasn't in danger. He wasn't trying to bite off part of your body."

"He wasn't trying to bite you. He was just barking because he didn't know you. He was guarding the house. That's what dogs do."

"Yeah, well, I didn't notice him barking at you."

"That's because I have a sweet, innocent, friendly face."

"So what are you saying? That I don't?"

"Well... if the proof is in the pudding..."

Bridge got down off the counter. "What profound thing are you gonna say next... if the shoe fits..."

"No, I'll leave the nerd stuff to you. Fits you better."

They walked out of the kitchen and into the living room. They heard a moan, then looked over at the couch and saw the man start to move around. Nicole sighed, not really wanting to have to hit him again.

"Can you do the honors this time? My foot's still aching from the last couple times."

Bridge looked at her, then shrugged. He wasn't against putting a whooping on the man, especially for looking at his girlfriend the way he was picturing in his mind. He walked over to the couch, then pulled his arm back as far as it could go, then released it like it was on a recoil. The punch landed flush across the man's cheek, sending him spiraling down to the floor again.

"Wow. Hit him kinda hard there, didn't you?"

Bridge didn't see the issue. "You told me to take care of it."

"OK, let's just hurry up and get this over with before the cavalry comes."

"Who else would be coming?"

"I don't know. I don't know if anyone other than this guy takes care of the place or not. Our conversation didn't get that in-depth."

"You got just about…"

"Don't say it," Nicole said. "If you know what's good for you, and you want me to be in a good mood later at the hotel, don't say it."

Bridge took another look at her. With how sexy she was looking, there was no sarcastic comment in the world worth losing that later. He quickly buttoned his mouth. "Let's take separate rooms. It'll be faster."

"Be on the lookout for other alarms or traps."

"And look for wall or floor safes first."

The two then split up, each taking a separate room of the house. Bridge started with the living room, while Nicole checked out the first bedroom she encountered. They turned the place upside down, and while they weren't sure they would find the diamonds or even think it was likely they were there, they couldn't rule it out either. If they couldn't find the diamonds, they would settle for anything else that looked interesting. A slip of paper with some names on it that Machado worked with, including one that had ties to Drewiskie. A folder detailing some of Machado's business. Financial statements. Bank account numbers. Anything they could use to their advantage would come in handy. Once they were done with their separate rooms, they each continued on, both of them taking another bedroom.

"Anything yet?" Bridge asked, entering the bedroom.

"Not yet."

A few more minutes went by, but nothing of interest was found. Then Nicole looked behind a picture on the wall and saw a safe embedded into the wall.

"Luke!" Nicole shouted.

Bridge immediately came running, seeing Nicole remove the picture from the wall as he came in. He instantly sized the safe up, determining what he needed. Nicole went back into the living room and grabbed his backpack, which had some of the tools of the trade in it. Bridge was a master locksmith. Part of his duties as a foreign agent in the CIA had been breaking into safes, vaults, and other locked up devices. Even after leaving the agency, he kept up with modern methods of breaking into devices. And he knew them all. He could punch, peel, drill, tunnel, scope, use brute-force, manipulate the lock, as well as use an autodialer, which was his personal favorite since that used the least amount of effort.

Unlike how it was sometimes depicted in the movies, there was no easy way to get into a safe. They were all time-consuming. The only question was how much time a person had to get into it. That usually determined the method. In this case, he decided to use the autodialer. Now, in the movies, this safe would have been opened in a matter of seconds with an autodialer. But in reality, it could take up to twenty-four hours depending on the device used. Luckily, Bridge used an autodialer that was specifically engineered for the CIA and wasn't on the market for regular users. It could open a safe in about fifteen to twenty minutes. If he was in a hurry, he could have tried to drill, but that would have taken some time too. Most of the modern safes had relocking mechanisms once a person drilled into it, and this safe looked to be the latest and greatest, as one would expect Machado to have.

Once Bridge had the autodialer in place, he and Nicole continued searching the house. Hopefully by the time they were looking through the other rooms, they would come back to the safe, and the combination would be known. There were a couple more rooms to be looked through, but none of them would reveal anything of importance. After the twenty minutes were up, they returned to the room with the safe. Bridge looked on the autodialer, seeing the combination to the safe in big red numbers.

Bridge smiled. "Love this thing. These chumps that have the autodialers on the market and have to wait half the day for the combo have no idea what they're missing."

"Guess working for a top-secret clandestine agency has its advantages after all."

"It does indeed."

"I'm surprised they let you keep some of the stuff you have though," Nicole remarked. "I would've thought they would have wanted some of it back."

"Who says they did?"

"You mean they didn't?"

"The CIA doesn't exactly like having civilians walk around with some of their toys, you know."

Nicole raised her eyebrows. "You stole them?!"

"Don't be ridiculous. Everything they wanted back, I gave back. It's just that, over the years, you start acquiring things off the books, off the official records, and you just start storing them in different places around the world in case you need them one day in your retirement. Or in other unofficial duties."

"You sly dog."

"It's really no different from what any other agent would do, or has done, or will do. Everyone does it."

"Including having different bank accounts?"

"I told you, every secret agent has several different bank accounts, usually that are untraceable. Just in case the time comes when the man decides you're no longer useful to them, or tries to eliminate you somehow, you don't have to work a nine-to-five like the normal people out there."

"Oh, can't have that. Can't be like the normal people."

"I don't mean it in a negative light," Bridge said. "But let's face it. People like us... we're not normal."

"You maybe. Not me. I'm as normal as can be."

"Oh yeah, right. You who flies around in helicopters with bazookas and RPGs. Yeah. Totally normal."

"That was in the line of duty."

"Right."

Bridge got back to the business at hand and unlocked the safe. He opened it and started removing the contents. It looked like the normal stuff. Papers, files, a few pieces of jewelry. He handed everything off to Nicole, who placed it on the desk as she started looking through it all. The last thing Bridge saw in there was a small wooden box. He removed it and put it on the desk. Bridge looked at Nicole, thinking this could be it. It was a small mahogany box. It sure looked like something that could hold a bunch of diamonds in it.

"This might be it," Bridge said.

"So open it."

"Hold on."

Bridge leaned down, his eyes level with the desk as

he inspected the box. Nicole then did the same, wondering what he was looking at.

"Uh, is there a problem?"

"Making sure there's no tricks that come along with this," Bridge replied.

"What tricks? What tricks could there possibly be?"

"Spoken like someone who's never been in the field."

"Excuse me?"

"I don't mean now. I mean in the CIA. You had a desk and a chair."

"I think I've gotten plenty of experience these last few years with you."

"Of course you have," Bridge said, meaning no offense. "All I meant was... look, one time I was on a mission in Iraq. I was sent to retrieve this box out of the quarters of a high-ranking officer from a joint task police force because they suspected him of having allegiances with a terrorist leader. Anyway, I got the box... it actually looked somewhat similar to this. A little darker in color. But anyway, the box was locked, obviously, so I picked the lock open, and when I opened it, some type of poisonous nerve agent was released into the air. Obviously placed there in case someone tampered with it."

"So that's what's wrong with you, huh? You got gassed? Poisoned?"

Bridge took his eyes off the box and looked at his partner. "Really?"

Nicole laughed. "Obviously you made it out in time."

"Luckily I wasn't standing with my face in front of it or else I would've been dead in thirty seconds."

"How were you standing then?"

"Kind of like to the side." Bridge then repositioned the box on the desk. "Kind of like this."

"Oh."

"Might as well open it like this since I already moved it."

Bridge put his hand on the front of the box and tried to open it, but it was locked. He removed a thin piece of wire from his pocket and picked the lock, getting the job done in just a few seconds. He then stood to the side of the box and cautioned Nicole to do the same. He slowly opened it, his head leaning back in case another mysterious toxin was released into the air. After opening it all the way, there was no mysterious gas or smoke released, much to Bridge's relief. He and Nicole looked into the box, seeing a small pouch, the kind that would hold a bunch of diamonds in it.

Bridge grabbed hold of the pouch and removed it from the box. He held it in the air, moving it up and down to get a feel for its weight. Seemed about right. He gave Nicole a look, like he thought they might have actually found what they were looking for. Nicole then felt the pouch as well, agreeing that it seemed like the right amount of weight. Bridge put the pouch on the desk, turning it upside down to release the contents for both of them to see. Several diamonds came tumbling out, rolling free onto the desk. But both Bridge and Nicole couldn't hide the look of disappointment from their faces. They were diamonds, but not the ones they were looking for. Bridge took out a picture of the diamonds, just to compare, but they were obviously not the right ones. These were much smaller, and though they undoubtedly were worth a fortune, Bridge guessed they would come in right around the million dollar mark, a little lower than the ones they were looking for.

"What now?" Nicole asked.

"Back to the drawing board, I guess."

"We could still take these. Maybe Drewiskie would settle for replacements."

"You know as well as I do that he doesn't want replacements. He wants the real deal. Besides, we don't even know for sure that Machado's the one who took them. He might be completely innocent of these charges. We'd just be stealing from one guy to give to another."

"Well, let's be honest, it's not like we'd be taking them from a saint or something. Machado is a pretty bad dude."

"Agreed," Bridge said. "But he's also a pretty bad dude we don't need issues with if we can avoid it."

"True."

They rounded up everything they took out of the safe and put it back in. They were careful not to make a mess of the place, not wanting it to look like there was a robbery or anything. With the power cutting out, all the cameras were also out of commission, so that meant there would be no trace of them ever being there, outside of the knocked-out man in the living room. And if nothing was disturbed, and nothing was missing, he was unlikely to ever tell Machado about what happened. He wouldn't want to out himself like that and get an earful about getting played by a beautiful woman. As long as everything was the same when they left as when they entered, it would be considered no harm, no foul by everybody.

Bridge and Nicole went back through every room, checking it twice, and also making sure they didn't leave any trace of their presence. Everything was in the same condition as when they found it. Nicole had also made sure to pick up her device on the electric panel, not wanting to leave it behind. Once they were done, they went back into the living room. The man started moaning while he was on the floor. He put his arms on the floor to brace and balance himself, as if he was about to do some push-ups. Nicole quickly walked over to him and delivered another well-timed and well-placed kick across his face, sending him crashing to the floor once again.

Bridge chuckled to himself. "He's gonna have one nasty headache when he wakes up."

"He's lucky he's waking up at all."

Bridge put the backpack on his back and started

walking to the door. "Well, I guess that wraps it up here."

"Oh, wait." Nicole started going through the house again.

"What are you doing?"

"I'm gonna let the dog in again."

"Oh no, you're not. Not while I'm here!"

Bridge immediately ran out of the house, not stopping until he was safely off the property, closing the front gate after he went through it. A couple of minutes later, Nicole came walking down the driveway, seeing her partner on the other side of the fence.

"You really couldn't wait for me?"

"Not when you unleash that beast," Bridge answered.

"He's not a beast. He's a very friendly dog."

"Yeah, well, I got a few body parts that think otherwise."

Nicole pulled the gate open and then went through it, closing it behind her. "Oh stop, he didn't even bite you."

"He wanted to!"

"You're such a drama queen, and he did not. He was just barking because he didn't know you."

The two then started walking back to their car.

"I saw teeth!" Bridge said. "Whenever you see a dog's teeth, that means they mean business."

"It does not. Stop being a delicate little flower."

Bridge didn't bother responding to the comment as

they reached the car. Once they put their stuff back in, he took another look at his girlfriend, remembering their promise from earlier.

"Are we, uh, still on for later?"

Nicole smiled. "You think you can handle it?"

"Can I handle it? Can you handle it? Are you up for round two?"

"Only round two? I'm up to going the distance if you got the stamina. All twelve rounds."

Bridge smiled and leaned in to kiss her. "I like the sound of that."

10

Once Bridge and Nicole woke up, they showered together, got dressed and had breakfast. They immediately went to work on what they were going to do next. As Nicole did some work on the computer, Bridge called their client to keep him informed on the events that had transpired.

"Well, we got into Machado's place in Los Angeles. There's no diamonds there."

"Are you sure?" Drewiskie asked.

"Positive. We turned the place inside out, upside down, and every other corny phrase you can think of. It wasn't there. We even broke into his safe and found some diamonds, but they weren't yours."

"Maybe he disguised them somehow."

"No, these were smaller than yours. Shaped differently."

"That's disappointing."

"I know. Machado wasn't there, however. Supposedly, he's out of town."

"What are you going to do now?"

"Well, he's got a place down in Brazil," Bridge answered. "That's probably going to be our next move."

"And if that doesn't work?"

"Well, one thing at a time. If he really does have the diamonds, and they're not in L.A., then they gotta be in Brazil. He's only got two homes."

"Unless he put them in a safe deposit box or a bank or something."

"Well, I guess that's something we can look at if we don't come up with anything here."

"They gotta be there. They just have to be," Drewiskie said.

"There's also the possibility that he doesn't have them at all. It's entirely possible someone else took them."

"But who? You said yourself you've checked the bank accounts of everyone I've been in contact with, and there's nothing unusual there. If someone close to me took them and sold them, wouldn't they have an unusual amount of money in there?"

"Not unless they opened up a special account under another name just for this purpose. Or if they haven't actually sold the diamonds yet."

Drewiskie loudly sighed into the phone. "This is ridiculous. Not you, just this whole situation."

"I know it's frustrating, but that's why you hired me.

One way or another, I'm gonna figure out what happened and who took them. Might take a little longer than we figured, but I promise you I'm gonna find them."

"Well, thank you. It's at least a little comforting to know that you're on the case."

Once Bridge was off the phone, he snuck up behind his girlfriend and put his arms around her, kissing her on the neck. She immediately stopped what she was doing and enjoyed the moment.

"Mmm, that feels so good." Bridge then sat beside her. "No, don't stop."

"Have to. Got work to do."

"Ugh. You always bring that up."

"Work before play."

"You always say that too."

"So what are we looking at?"

"Already booked us a flight to Rio tonight," Nicole answered.

"What time?"

"Ten."

"How long?"

"Thirteen hours. No stops."

"I hate long flights," Bridge said.

"It was the shortest they had."

"I know, but I still hate long flights."

Before packing for the trip, Bridge called a contact of his in Brazil to make sure they would have some supplies they needed for when they got down there.

MIKE RYAN

Mostly guns, weapons, and some of the other illegal items you weren't supposed to fly with. Though it was possible sometimes to slip a few of those things past the security screeners at the airport, and Bridge knew a few tricks to make that even more likely, it wasn't worth the hassle if it failed. With all the years he put in at the CIA, he had contacts all over the world. Many of which he still kept up-to-date with from time to time. In his business, it was always nice to know people. He would need them every now and again.

Once he was done talking to his contact, Nicole came over to him.

"Everything all set?"

"We're good to go," Bridge replied. "All that's left to do now is have a little fun in the sun."

Nicole shook her head. "That's not all that's left to do."

"It's not?" Bridge looked perplexed, wondering what he forgot.

The only thing he'd forgotten, though, was her. Nicole looked at him playfully until he finally got the message. "What on earth could we do with our time before we have to leave?"

"Uh..."

Nicole pushed him down on the bed, then pulled her top off, revealing she wasn't wearing a bra. "Like you said, it's gonna be a long flight. We might as well tire ourselves out so we can sleep on it."

Bridge smiled, admiring his girlfriend's chest. "I'll,

uh..." He never finished his sentence, and instead, started kissing Nicole all over.

They flew into Galeao International Airport. It was about twelve miles north of downtown Rio de Janeiro. Machado's residence was in the Rua Jackson de Figueiredo area, which was roughly a fifty-minute drive from the airport. Before going out to do reconnaissance on Machado's house, Bridge and Nicole first checked into a hotel that was along the route.

While Nicole set her computers up and got them running, Bridge unpacked their belongings. After their things were settled, Bridge then left the hotel alone, to meet his contact and get the supplies they needed, including a few weapons. He got back to the hotel a little over an hour after leaving. When he came back, he found Nicole at the desk, typing away.

"Everything go OK?"

Bridge put his black bag on the bed. "All according to plan."

"Get what we need?"

"Yep. A couple pistols, two assault rifles, ammo, a couple wetsuits, and..."

"Wetsuits?"

"Well, Machado's got a beachfront house, right?"

"Yeah?"

"We might have to get in through alternative

measures," Bridge replied with a smile, actually kind of looking forward to going into a house through different means than the front door. Or back door. "Kind of neat, huh?"

"Oh. Yeah. Totally looking forward to it."

"How's it going on your front?"

"Found some pictures of Machado's place," Nicole said. "There's actually a bunch still on the internet from the sale."

"When was that?"

"Sold a little over a year ago for seven and a half million."

Bridge whistled. "That's a pretty good chunk of change."

"Gets even nicer. There's eight rooms, eleven bathrooms, a hundred-and-eighty-degree view of the city, the ocean, the beaches of Sao Conrado and Ipanema, as well as the forest of Tijuca, and the Cagarras Islands."

Along with everything Nicole mentioned, it was also a three-story building, with balconies on the second and third levels, overlooking the in-ground pool, the beach, and the ocean.

"I guess it sounds all right," Bridge said. "You know, for more modest people."

"Oh, almost forgot, there's also a small helipad, along with a tennis court."

"Is that all?" Bridge asked, sounding unimpressed. "No soccer fields on the premises?"

"Uh, no. They couldn't quite fit that in."

"I'd take a hard pass on it then. Doesn't sound like anything I'd ever be comfortable with."

Bridge went over to the desk so Nicole could show him the pictures of the house. After they discussed the beautiful interior of the home, Bridge stopped joking around and thought of all the problems they might encounter. And there were plenty of them.

"What are you thinking?" Nicole asked.

"I'm thinking I'd like to bypass this whole thing."

"I meant, what are you reasonably thinking?"

"That I'd like to bypass this whole thing."

"Well, obviously that's not a reasonable request."

"I'm thinking that's a lot of rooms for one guy," Bridge said.

"You think he's got an army in there?"

"Sounds a lot bigger than his place in L.A."

"It is. There's an extra two thousand square feet."

Bridge blew some air through his lips, not liking the setup. "A helipad, eight rooms, in-ground pool, tennis courts; that sounds like a lot of maintenance to me. Something you'll need a lot of help with for the upkeep."

"And I doubt he's doing any of that himself."

"You don't buy a place for seven million then mow your own lawn and skim the pool yourself."

"I don't think we're getting into this place as easily as the last place," Nicole said.

"I think you're right about that."

"It's gonna require a lot more surveillance."

Bridge smiled. "That's what I love. More surveillance."

They started working out plans, figuring this wasn't going to be a one- or two-day affair. They were going to be there for probably a week, if not longer. They determined there were three ways to go as far as getting more intel on the house. One was the usual way, sitting outside in a car, documenting everyone who went in or out. The second was by air. They could circle up above the place, taking pictures in a helicopter. That would be more to get a layout of the property. It wouldn't really help as far as figuring out how many people were usually inside. The third way was to get a boat and take some pictures from the water. That might be useful in both respects. They could get a layout of the land and see how many people were outside.

"So what do you wanna do?" Nicole asked.

"All of it. We can't afford mistakes here. Not with a guy like Machado. This place is probably going to be heavily guarded, heavily armed, security systems, alarms, cameras, you name it, he's probably got it. Can't take chances. We need to know for a fact what we're dealing with here."

"You don't think I could do the same bit here as back in L.A.?"

"Uh, no. For one, if by chance that guy called down here, you're as good as dead before you ever step foot in that building. And two, you don't exactly look like you would work for the Brazilian electric company."

"I could, uh, try some other ways," Nicole said seductively.

"No! No other ways. We're gonna do this from a distance this time. We're not getting up close and personal."

"We're not?" Nicole sat on his lap.

"Well, uh, they aren't. We are."

11
───────

After Bridge and Nicole were done with their hanky-panky, they got started on the task at hand. They drove down to Machado's place, parking well down the street, far enough where they would be away from being spotted on any cameras, but where they could still see the entrance to the house. It turned out to be a quiet night, with not much going on. They stayed at it, late into the night, before finally going back to the hotel.

The next morning, they repeated the activity. With one exception. This time, Bridge was by himself in the car and Nicole was up in a helicopter taking pictures. They figured they could save time by doing it this way and splitting up. Plus, Bridge wasn't all that fond of helicopters. He wasn't fearful of them, and would go up in them if he had to, like he did in Mexico, but flying in them wasn't exactly his favorite thing to do.

Especially hovering over a building and taking pictures. That was more Nicole's thing. She had no qualms about doing that. Bridge preferred to fly via a plane if he had to travel by air, although short trips by helicopter were all right. But just hovering over a building, he had issues with that.

It probably had something to do with his time in the CIA. He had a similar situation, taking pictures for the government, trying to locate a terrorist cell group, when suddenly the helicopter he was in started taking fire. A few minutes later, the tail rotor got clipped from a rocket, sending the chopper spiraling. Luckily, the pilot was somehow able to put the bird down safely, though they still wound up in enemy territory. Bridge and the pilot were stranded for three days in a mountainous region without any support other than a couple of pistols that they brought with them. Obviously, he made it out unscathed, but it wasn't an easy time. And he never forgot it. So whenever a mission called for a helicopter staying in one spot for a period of time, he was more than willing to let Nicole have at it. He was OK flying in a chopper if it was moving from point A to point B, but hovering, hovering made him shiver.

As Bridge sat there in the car, he waited to see the helicopter overhead. They were in communication the entire morning, though he left it up to her to figure out how she was getting the chopper. Whether she stole one, rented one, or bought one, it was all up to her. In reality, it wasn't that difficult. She found a helicopter, and a pilot, who didn't have an issue flying over a small area for a little amount of time for a big amount of money. All Nicole told the pilot was that she was taking some nature and geography photos for a world magazine. Pictures of the coast, the beach, the ocean. She was in the back seat, and his eyes were on flying, so he wouldn't be in much of a position to actually see what she was shooting at, anyway.

"Almost there, Luke. Probably about five minutes out."

Bridge looked up at the sky, though he still didn't see anything. "Good. Be careful up there."

"I think we'll be fine. I don't think we'll be dodging any RPGs up here."

"You never know. You're not exactly going to be filming a monastery, you know. A guy like Machado might have defense mechanisms in place. He sees a chopper hovering overhead, he might let loose."

Nicole thought he was overreaching, though she understood his concerns. She was well aware of his issues about the hovering helicopter, him telling her the story in detail not long after they initially got together after leaving the CIA. But regardless of that, she was always prepared, even if she didn't believe anything would happen.

"No need to worry about it," Nicole said. "Nothing's going to happen. But if it does, I got it."

Bridge was silent for a second, trying to figure out what that meant. "You got it? You got what?"

"I got it covered."

It then came to Bridge suddenly. He knew what she meant. "You didn't."

"Didn't what?"

"Did you bring a cannon on that chopper?"

Nicole laughed. "What?! Of course not!"

Bridge didn't believe her. "Nic, I know you. What did you do?"

"I didn't do anything. All I've got here is a camera."

"And?"

"And a little black bag of stuff."

Bridge closed his eyes, almost afraid of what he was going to hear. "What's in it?"

"Uh, just a little protection should I need it."

"What do you have with you? Bazookas, grenades, RPGs, cannons, rifles, bombs, explosives, what?"

"Don't be silly. I couldn't fit a bazooka or RPG in this bag."

"I noticed you left the other things out of your denial."

"Well, I might have a few little trinkets, just to be safe."

"And just what are you planning to do if you get fired upon?"

"I'm gonna tell the pilot to move in closer so I can drop some grenades," Nicole replied. "That'll get the party started really quick. Then while they're ducking for cover on the ground, I can assemble the rifle and start picking them off."

"Oh my god, you are such a danger to society. I love you for it, but there's something crazy about you. The CIA missed their mark when they had you sitting behind a desk. You should've been in the field."

"That's what I always told them."

"Well, let's hope we don't start bombing Baghdad here, and it's a nice peaceful afternoon."

"See anything on your end yet?"

"I've seen a few people come and go," Bridge answered. "Haven't seen Machado yet, though."

Another minute later and Bridge could finally see the helicopter come into view. Nicole only needed to hover over the property for a few minutes, and maybe not even that long. She just needed to get a few clear shots of the grounds. While the helicopter was over-head, Bridge split his concentration between the air and looking at the front gate. He almost expected to see a rocket launched into the air any second, its sights set on the helicopter. It was just his paranoia playing with him, though, as that missile never came. Three minutes later and the helicopter was on its way, back to where it came from like nothing ever happened. Bridge let out a sigh, thankful the whole event was without incident, though he really knew there was unlikely to be anything to begin with. Still, he breathed a bit easier.

"How'd you make out up there?"

"Good," Nicole replied. "Got all the shots we needed."

"I didn't hear any explosions."

"See? And you thought every time I was in a helicopter that something blew up."

"First time for everything."

"What do you want me to do after I land? Come out to you?"

"Or I can pick you up?"

"Probably shouldn't leave and risk missing something. I can just take a taxi and have him drop me off up the street from you."

"Sounds good."

"Unless you want me to just rent a boat. Then I can just slip on my bikini and relax out on the water."

"You're gonna be alone on a boat, in a bikini? Uh, no! If you're gonna be on a boat in a bikini, I want to be there too."

"Well, I didn't say I was going to be alone," Nicole teased. "Maybe there will be a nice, handsome, young boat captain who's willing to go out there with me." There was silence on the other end of the phone for a good long while. "I'm just kidding you know."

"Oh, good. I wasn't mad or anything. It was just, I was having trouble talking because the phone was sticking to my ear from the steam that was coming out of my head."

Nicole laughed. "You know you're the only one for me."

"So you say."

"So is true. So what do you want me to do?"

"I guess just come out to the car with me."

"Why? You wanna get a little busy in the back seat?"

"Business, Nic, business. Let's remember why we're here, shall we?"

"What would be blending in more than two tourists going at it in the backseat of a car in a beautiful country?"

"Uh, you really want me to answer that?"

"Besides, we could set the camera up and shoot video continuously so we don't have to watch. We can then play the tape later."

"You're so bad."

"Bad in a good way or bad in a bad way?"

"Bad in a Nicole way."

"You know you love it though."

"I can't deny that," Bridge said.

"You don't like my bikini and a boat idea?"

"Not without me."

"So let's do it."

"I think maybe tomorrow or the day after. I wanna get one or two solid days sitting out here first. This is where people are coming and going. I doubt they're entering from the ocean."

"Never know," Nicole said.

"Just get down here, and we'll figure it out when you get here."

"Ooh, that sounds like it might be..."

"Nothing dirty. Get your mind out of the gutter for a change."

"Why? It's a pleasant place to be."

Bridge laughed. He wasn't sure if she always meant what she said, talking about sex, hinting about sex, but it always seemed to lift up their moods and relieve any tension they may have been feeling. Maybe that was why she did it. Maybe it was a ploy by her to not get too focused on a mission that they missed what was right in front of them.

"Should I go commando for our back-seat mission?" Nicole asked.

Bridge snickered. "Just get down here."

"Down there? Already preparing for me, are we?"

"Oh my... you can turn anything into a sexual comment, can't you?"

"I dunno. I can sure try!"

"Just get... here, as fast as you can."

"On my way, sir!"

Bridge kept laughing, long after his conversation with Nicole was over. He kept his eyes on the front of Machado's property, observing a car pull up. Two men stepped out. Neither was Machado, though. Both of these men looked tough. Beefy looking. Like the kind he would have to deal with before this mission was over. The prospect did not excite him.

12

After four days of surveillance on the front of Machado's house, Bridge thought they had a good enough idea of what was going on out there. Who was coming, who was going, and how long they were staying there. Along with the pictures that Nicole took from the air, they were beginning to get a good idea about what was going on in the property. But it wasn't complete yet. There was still one area that they wanted a better visual on, and that was the back. That they could do via a boat.

Nicole had rented something, a walkaround boat, often called a cuddy. It was meant to be a fishing boat because of its ability to fish from anywhere along the boat, thanks to a passway around the boat from the stern all the way to the bow. It was a thirty-foot vessel, complete with a small cabin with a toilet, along with a roof overhead of the main seating area as well as for whoever was steering. The back of the boat was exposed to the elements, but had a small bench seating area. The boat was designed for fishing, but also had some speed to it to cover longer distances if desired.

The plan was to dock a few miles offshore, then take some pictures of the back of Machado's house. They brought some fishing gear with them—also rented—just to give the appearance they were innocent fishermen. They were still about twenty minutes away from the spot they had figured on, with Bridge steering the boat. He was in a tank top and shorts, giving off the vibe of a fisherman beach enthusiast. Nicole was also in shorts and a tank top, though she was about to change into something more comfortable too. She began taking off her clothes, loudly clearing her throat to make sure Bridge would turn around to look at her. He did, observing her just in time to see her removing her shorts. She was completely naked and she didn't seem to be in a hurry to cover up.

"What are you doing?!"

"Changing," Nicole answered innocently.

"Uh... we're out in the open, you know."

Nicole looked around. "Umm, I don't see anyone else, do you?"

Bridge looked around, not seeing another boat that was close enough in the distance to see the debauchery that was going on in theirs. He turned his head to make sure he wasn't crashing into anything, even though there was nothing in front of him except water, but he also slowed the boat down so he could look back at his stunning girlfriend. His mind was telling him to get back to the wheel and keep going, but everything else was telling him to keep looking. Especially his eyes. They weren't going anywhere other than Nicole's body.

Nicole enjoyed the attention he gave her, sitting down on the seat, not modest at all. But why should she? She had a nice-looking figure, and Bridge had seen it all before, and there was no one else within seeing distance. It was the first time she'd been alone on a boat to do something like this. And she was taking advantage of it.

"Should I, uh, cover up?"

Bridge looked at her with lust in his eyes. Everything was telling him to get back to the mission. Business first. That's what he always said. Business first. But it sure was hard to think about business when he had a beautiful, naked woman right in front of him. The sun was beating down; it was warm, and there was no one else around. All the ingredients necessary to have a little fun in the sun.

"You should," Bridge said, not really meaning a word of it. "You should."

"Oh." Nicole got up, making sure he got an even better view. "I guess I'll put some clothes on then."

"You should. But I don't want you to."

Nicole walked over to him, rubbing her body against his. As she took his shorts off, Bridge turned the motor off, not wanting the boat to run away from them and really crash into something while they were busy. They went down into the small cabin of the boat and found a small, not really comfortable couch. But it was good enough for what they were doing.

They emerged from the cabin forty-five minutes later, neither having any clothes on. Bridge quickly found his and got dressed again, while Nicole went into her bag and removed a small two-piece bikini. After she got dressed, Bridge looked at her, still enamored with her figure. It was one of those bikinis that barely had enough fabric to cover any portion of her body, and really didn't. A micro G-string bikini bottom it was called, where her ass was hanging out of it so much it was a wonder why she bothered to put one on at all. It was really only meant to cover the front, and even that was questionable. The top she had on was the triangle mini-top style, where the fabric only covered the nipples, with the rest of her breasts almost bulging out. Well, they were bulging out in all directions.

"What's the point of those?" Bridge asked, starting the boat up again.

"What?"

Bridge pointed at her. "Those. Those bikinis. I mean, they don't cover a thing. What's the point of wearing them?"

"Are you complaining?"

"No, not at all. I'm just asking from a man's point of

view. Don't get me wrong, I love it, I'm just asking, when you're wearing that little, and it's barely covering anything, is there really a point?"

"Because I like it and it's comfortable."

"It can't be that comfortable."

"It's a way to cover yourself and still be legal, how's that?"

"I'll accept that."

"Sounds like you're complaining," Nicole said.

"Believe me, I'm not."

After Nicole adjusted her bikini, she walked back over to Bridge, standing behind him and fondling him.

"Uh, Nic, at some point, we really do need to work."

"We've got the boat rented for the day. Might as well put it to good use."

"Is there a reason why we just got dressed? I have a feeling that might be a repeated theme throughout the day," Bridge said.

"If you're lucky, it will be."

After a few minutes, Bridge stopped fighting it, and just accepted what was about to come. Not that it wasn't pleasurable. He turned off the boat again as they both tumbled down to the floor, beginning round two. Thirty minutes later, they returned to their former positions, with Bridge steering the boat. He only put shorts on this time, figuring he'd make it easier for the next time, positive there would be a next time. Nicole slipped on her bikini again, though Bridge still wondered why she bothered. He figured it was just to tease him. It worked. It was tough focusing with her looking like that. But somehow, he managed. Bridge looked at the time.

"Oh my god, it's only ten o'clock in the morning, and I already feel exhausted."

Nicole smiled, proud of herself. "Nice, isn't it?"

Bridge laughed. "You are such a nymphomaniac."

"Are you complaining?"

"Not at all!"

"Sure sounds like it sometimes. I mean, I think a lot of guys would love to have a girlfriend who is so easy to please."

"I'm not at all complaining." Bridge leaned over and kissed her on the lips.

"You love it. You just like to give the appearance that you don't and are difficult."

Bridge smiled. "I won't confirm nor deny anything."

Once they finally got to a spot they were comfortable with, about ten miles offshore of Machado's place, they stopped the boat and got out their fishing gear. They put their fishing rods into the holders on the edge of the boat, then sat down on the bench and got out their binoculars. Nicole stared at him for a moment.

"What?" Bridge asked.

"Are those new?"

Bridge looked at his binoculars. "Yeah. Got them about a month ago."

"They look nice."

"Better be nice for nine hundred bucks."

Nicole whistled. "That's a hefty price tag."

"Would be if that's what I paid for them. I only paid about four fifty."

"Fell off the back of the truck, huh?"

Bridge laughed. "I, uh, went shopping at Martin's. He called me up, said he had some new merchandise come in."

"I still don't know why you bother with that guy. You know all that stuff is stolen."

"He's got good prices. He's fast. And he's dependable."

"I think there's some retail stores that would disagree with you. You're helping to keep guys like him in business."

"If it wasn't me buying, it would be somebody else."

"That's not a great argument."

"Didn't say it was. Just said it was my reasoning."

"Still..."

"Can we just get back to what we're here for and look at Machado's place?"

"Sure." Nicole looked at him again. "Are those waterproof?"

Bridge sighed and took the binoculars away from his face and looked at his girlfriend. "Yes, they're waterproof. And they have a high-powered lens that you could see the moon with. Should I go over all the specs with you?"

"No, I'm good."

"Thank you."

"You can really see the moon with them?"

Bridge took a deep breath. "Nicole."

"OK, OK, I'm done."

They sat there for the next six hours, looking through their binoculars, noting everyone they saw on the grounds, taking as many pictures as they could. Finally, they started getting hungry and figured it was time to bring the boat back. They brought a few snacks to tide them over, but it wasn't enough to keep their stomachs at bay. They started the boat back up and were about halfway back to the dock when Nicole got another idea. She came over to Bridge, putting her hands on him, hoping to delay getting back to shore for another hour or two.

"Uh, maybe we should, um, stay out on the boat for a little while longer."

"I thought you were getting hungry?" Bridge asked. He then looked over at his girlfriend and could tell by the look in her eye exactly what she meant. Nicole leaned back, thrusting her chest out.

"The boat doesn't need to be back for a few more hours. Might as well take advantage of it."

Bridge started thinking. It was hard not to be tempted by her. Darn near impossible, actually. "We're not getting back to shore anytime soon, are we?"

Nicole smiled. "Not if I can help it."

Bridge snickered. "I had a feeling."

Nicole then put her arms around Bridge's neck,

kissing his lips. "Actually, I think we should do this again tomorrow."

"You do, huh?"

"Absolutely. I mean, one day isn't really enough to see what's going on in there. We should give it at least one more, maybe even two, to make sure everything is consistent, and there are no surprises."

"We're gonna have to find another boat."

"No need. I already rented this one for tomorrow too."

Bridge smiled as he kissed her. "You already were planning all this, weren't you?"

"You always told me to be resourceful."

"I think I taught you too well."

"So what do you say? Should we camp out another day?"

Bridge kissed her on the lips. "How could I say no?"

13

Bridge and Nicole spent the next three days watching Machado's house, taking notes on everyone who went in. One of those days was spent on a boat, two in a car. After the fifth day, they believed they were ready to make their move. It was mostly the same people going in and out, believed to be bodyguards on Machado's payroll, or high-ranking members of his organization. They all looked the part. But there never seemed to be more than eight people in the house at any one time, not including a bunch of women who went in and had yet to leave. There were six of them.

"I don't like this," Nicole said, looking down at the plans that her partner had drawn.

"It's the best we're going to be able to do. We're not getting in the house unoccupied. There's gonna be people there. There's no two ways about it. That's just the way it is."

"But there are way too many people. I mean... I don't see how we can pull this off."

"The fewest number of people in there is around midnight. As far as we can tell, there's about four, right? Machado took off on his helicopter earlier today and hasn't come back, so we know he won't be there. That means security is probably the least we're gonna get. If we wait until Machado comes back, security's gonna double."

"I get all that. But I'm just saying, there's still a lot of bodies in there."

"Well, six of those bodies are female."

"And don't get any ideas."

"Judging by the clothes they were wearing when they came in, and seeing what they were doing from the boat, I don't think we need to worry about them. I doubt they're hiding any weapons under their bikini bottoms. Well, at least not the..."

"Don't say it," Nicole said.

"At least not the normal kind of weapon."

"You said it."

Bridge smiled, not able to help himself. "Sorry. Had to."

"Don't forget the alarms that you know they have set up."

"We'll be fine."

Nicole sighed and shook her head. "Luke..."

"I know. You don't like me going in by myself, but I'll be fine. You're outside for backup."

"I would think you would want me in there with you so we can get out of there faster. What am I gonna do waiting outside?"

"Look out for anybody who might be coming."

"So you're just gonna take care of everything inside by yourself?"

"That's the plan."

"The plan stinks."

"It will work. I'll take care of everyone inside. You make sure I'm not surprised while I'm in there."

It was a few minutes before midnight when Bridge and Nicole finally arrived at the Machado place. Well, they were actually a few minutes down the road, not wanting to set up shop right in front and advertise their arrival. Bridge took his gear, gun in hand, back-pack on his back, and slipped between a couple of other beachfront houses to make his way down to the golden sand along the ocean. He was going to attack Machado's house from the rear. Nicole sat in the car and watched the front, making sure nobody new came around. She had a bunch of her toys on the seat next to her. A shotgun, assault rifle, pistol, a couple grenades, and a taser. She was well prepared in case of emergency.

Bridge snuck across the shoreline until he came across the edge of Machado's property. He knelt down on one knee as he surveyed the area. He knew there was a guard back there and waited to see his outline. Instead, he saw a very different outline. Instead of a six-foot-two, two-hundred-and-twenty-pound guard, he saw a slender, attractive, black-haired beauty in a white bikini slowly walking down from the house to the beach. Bridge kept tabs on her for a few moments and saw her slipping out of her two-piece bathing suit. The woman stepped into the ocean and swam for the next ten minutes. Bridge's concentration on the woman was distracted by the other beautiful woman talking in his ear.

"Are you in yet?" Nicole asked.

Bridge touched his earpiece. "Not yet. Slight complication back here."

"Oh no, already?"

"One of the women is out here swimming."

"So forget her. Slip in while she's out there. Now you don't have to worry about her."

"Except when she comes in and finds me snooping around or something."

"What is she, a hundred and ten pounds? I'm sure you can deal with it. You can't be wasting time out there."

"I know. I'll give her three more minutes, then I'm in."

"Make sure you're looking at the right things."

Bridge then looked at the ocean again, seeing the woman emerge from the water. "Uh, well, I, uh, have her in sight again. She, uh, went in with no clothes on."

"She what?"

"I believe skinny-dipping is the term."

"Do I need to come back there and open a can of whoop-ass?"

"I don't think that'll be necessary."

"Luke, it's gonna be hard to move with a couple of broken legs."

Bridge laughed. "I'm not at all interested. She doesn't have anywhere near the figure that you do."

"You bought yourself a few more minutes."

"Carlos," the woman said as she walked on the sand, talking to the guard. "Can you bring me a towel?"

Bridge looked back to the grass and a small gate, seeing the guard emerge from the darkness. Bridge hid behind a large tree on the neighboring property and got out his tranquilizer gun. He wasn't interested in harming anyone permanently, but hitting them with a dart would be a lot easier than trying to fight them and then tie them up. As the guard walked on the beach, towel in hand, Bridge aimed his gun at the man's head. As soon as the guard handed the towel to the naked woman, Bridge fired his gun. The dart stuck in the man's neck, Carlos putting his hand up to it as he started to feel groggy. The woman screamed, seeing the man collapse right in front of him. That wasn't what Bridge was hoping for, because now he had to shut her up too, and fast, before she alerted anyone inside who was still awake.

Bridge aimed for her, hitting her in the stomach with a dart. She, too, instantly dropped to the ground.

The darts were laced with a moderate sedative,

powerful enough to knock someone out within seconds, and strong enough to keep them asleep for two to three hours. It was a technique he learned in the CIA. With those two people down, Bridge immediately ran toward the back of the property, going through a small metal gate that was open. Since it was already open with the other two at the beach, Bridge didn't have to worry about some type of alarm on it since it was likely off. Bridge ran past the tennis court and the helipad, then past the in-ground pool. Just as he got to the back of the house, he looked inside the glass doors and saw a man sitting in a chair, his back to the open windows. Bridge pointed his gun through the window and fired, his dart hitting the man in the back of the shoulder. The man stood up for a second, wondering what just hit him, but quickly fell to the ground.

Bridge then went over to the door, which was unlocked, and opened it. He heard a bunch of giggling coming from the next room over, which was the kitchen. Bridge froze, looking around to see where he could go. It turned out the answer was nowhere. The five women came into the room, holding a bunch of drinks and snacks, and all wearing little clothing. Two were in bikinis, and the other three were in some kind of lingerie. They all let out a little scream upon seeing the strange man standing there with a gun in his hands.

"Shh," Bridge said, putting his hand up to his lips.

"Who are you?" one of the ladies asked.

"Uhh..."

He didn't have time to answer, as one of the other guards came running into the room from the front of the house. Bridge immediately fired at the man before he could figure out what was happening, the dart hitting the man square in the chest. The man dropped to his knees, then slumped over.

"Oh my god, he's gonna kill all of us!" another of the women screamed.

"I'm not gonna kill you, just relax."

"He's gonna shoot us, oh my god!" the third woman yelled.

Bridge sighed and relaxed his shoulders. "Would you ladies relax?! This is a tranquilizer gun. He's not dead. He's just gonna be sleeping for a few hours. I'm not here to kill you."

"What are you here for?" the first woman asked, standing there in a red bikini.

Bridge almost forgot about the fourth guard in the house. He quickly remembered when he heard footsteps running down the stairs. Bridge rushed over to the steps, which came down facing a different direction than he was standing in, and waited for the guard to show his face. As soon as the guard got to the bottom of the steps and turned the corner, Bridge was waiting for him. All the guard saw was a gun pointing straight at him. He was quickly put to sleep when the dart lodged in his chest. The women started screaming again at seeing the last guard in the house fall violently to the ground. Bridge looked up to the ceiling and rolled his eyes. Bridge walked back over to them, none of them shutting up yet.

"Ladies!"

His yelling at them seemed to have no effect, as they continued screaming hysterically, afraid something was going to happen to them.

"Ladies!!" Bridge yelled at the top of his lungs, drowning out the women's voices. They all suddenly fell quiet. "That's better. I really hate shouting."

"Please don't kill us," the woman in the black lingerie said.

"I already told you, I'm not here to kill anybody. Now, you have two choices here. You can either be quiet, behave, sit down quietly, and cooperate, and I won't have to put you all to sleep, or you can continue to yell and carry on, in which case you're going to fall asleep one by one with the rest of these guys. Which will it be?"

The woman in the red bikini put her hand up. "May I ask a question?"

"We're not in school here. Just ask."

She pointed over to a white couch just next to Bridge's position. "Can we sit right there on the couch?"

Bridge smiled. "That would be fantastic."

The women all followed the red bikini's lead and hurried over to the couch and sat down, their hands on their knees as they waited for further instruction. She put her hand up again to ask another question.

"I told you, we're not in school here," Bridge said. "What do you want?"

"What happened to Inez?"

"Who's that?"

"She went out to go swimming."

"She wearing a white bikini?"

"Yes."

"She's currently sleeping, then."

The women put their hands on their mouths, afraid of what happened to their friend.

"Just relax," Bridge said. "She'll wake up in a couple hours, like nothing ever happened. She'll be fine."

The woman in the black lingerie, sitting on the end of the couch, stood up and let her clothing drop to the ground, standing there in all her glory. Bridge looked at her figure for a moment.

"Uh, what are you doing?" Bridge asked.

"I thought you were here for us. I just figured I would go first."

Bridge raised his eyebrows, then quickly shook his head, as if he was trying but failing to understand what was going on here. Bridge smiled, then put his gun back in its holster. He waved his hand at the woman to sit.

"Listen, ladies, you're all very attractive, very beautiful, but I'm not here for you. Any of you. First of all, I already have a beautiful girlfriend. Second, I'm here for diamonds."

"We have some upstairs," the one in the red bikini said.

"No, no, no, just listen to me, huh? I'll talk. You guys listen. I'm here for diamonds. Diamonds that I believe Machado has but doesn't own, and I'm here to get them back."

"Hector has many diamonds. He's a collector."

"I know. I'm here only for a special kind that I believe he took from someone that he shouldn't have." Bridge then reached into his backpack and removed a picture of the diamonds. He then gave it to the woman. "Have any of you seen these specific diamonds?"

The woman shook her head, then passed the picture along to her friends. One by one, they each took a look at the picture. And one by one, they each shook their heads, never having seen the diamonds before. After they were done, the naked woman handed the picture back to Bridge.

"None of you have ever seen these before?"

All the women shook their heads.

"Where does Machado keep his diamonds here?"

The women looked at each other, none of them wanting to be the one to reveal the location of Machado's diamonds.

"Listen, ladies, I'm kind of in a hurry here. Now, I can tear this whole house apart, and be here for a really long time, or you can tell me where it is, and then I can be out of here in a jiffy. Then you can get back to... whatever it is you were doing. Now what do you say?"

All the women looked to the woman in red, who seemed to be the unofficial leader of the group.

"Upstairs," the red bikini woman said. "In his office. He keeps all his jewelry in there."

"Very good. Now we're getting somewhere. Can you show me where that is?"

The woman nodded.

"Great. Now we're all going to get up and go upstairs to the office. I want everyone to be cool and relaxed and everything will be fine. If anyone freaks out, or tries to do anything, I'm gonna have to make you go night-night. Understood?"

All the women seemed to understand what he was saying. They got up and started walking away before Bridge quickly stopped them. He got next to the naked woman.

"Would you, uh, like to put your clothes back on before we go?"

The woman smiled at him and raised an eyebrow like she might be interested in him. "I'm good."

Bridge returned the smile, though a little more awkwardly than the one she gave. One by one, they all went over to the steps, Bridge the last one in line. They went up the stairs, then turned to the left, walking down the hall to Machado's office, which was the last room on the left. They went into the office, and the woman in the red bikini showed Bridge where Machado's safe was. It was hidden behind a picture on the wall.

"He needs to get more creative," Bridge said. "Same as L.A."

"What?"

"Nothing. Do you happen to know the combination to this?"

"Oh no. Hector doesn't give anyone the combination. Not even among the men he trusts. Only he knows."

Bridge smiled again. "Well, we'll just have to do something about that, won't we?"

He then reached into his backpack and removed the autodialer again, the same one that he used on the safe in L.A. He put it on the safe to get it going, then leaned up against the wall and stared at the women.

"This is gonna take a few minutes."

"What should we do now?"

"Just find yourselves a chair, the floor, sit down, make yourselves comfortable."

Everyone did as he directed, except the naked woman. She continued to stand there, not seeming the least bit bothered that she had no clothes. And with her body, Bridge could see why she wouldn't be ashamed of it.

"Uh, you can sit down too."

"We could always do something... more interesting as we wait," the woman said.

"Uh, yeah... no. No, we can't. Told you... the whole girlfriend thing. She wouldn't understand."

"But she is not here."

"Trust me, she would know. Thank you for the offer. You're very beautiful, and in another world, another life, believe me, I would be kicking myself for turning you down. But I'm afraid we'll have to stick to just business for now."

The woman then sat down, looking a little disappointed. "Maybe the next time you are in Brazil?"

"Uh, yeah, maybe."

Their conversation was interrupted by the sound of Nicole's voice in his ear. "How you making out in there?"

"Good. Good."

"Everyone eliminated?"

"Uh, well, yeah, kind of, sort of."

"Everyone's not been taken care of, have they?"

"Well... basically."

"Luke, stop talking in circles. Do you have everyone neutralized or not?"

"The guards are all down and out, yes."

Nicole could tell by the sound of his voice that something wasn't exactly the way it was supposed to be. "And the females?"

"They are... not an issue."

Nicole made a loud groan, already knowing what that meant. "You didn't tranq them, did you?"

"Uh, well, no, well, yeah, I did the one."

"And the rest?"

"They're being very cooperative."

"That better not mean what I think it means."

"Relax, they're all... uh..."

"Are they wearing clothes at least?"

"Um, well, one's not. And the rest are... very little."

"Luke!"

"They just showed me where Machado's safe is, so we're just waiting here until the combo is figured out."

"Waiting? And doing what while you're waiting?"

"Just talking."

"Luke."

Bridge could hear the anger in her voice starting to boil. He could just see her jaw line tensing up as she said his name.

"Just relax, everything's fine here. No one's doing any extracurricular activities. They're sitting calmly on the floor while we're waiting. Everything's fine."

Unfortunately, the waiting took longer than he figured. Unlike the safe in L.A., which only took about twenty minutes before the combination appeared, this one took an extra fifteen minutes. Once his machine beeped, Bridge snapped his head to it, clapping his hands that it was finally done. He went over to the safe and used the red numbers shown to unlock the safe. He opened it, then unloaded all the contents onto the desk. It was a bigger safe, with a lot more in it than the last one of Machado's that he'd opened.

Bridge started rooting through everything. There

were pouches, papers, jewelry, boxes, tons of stuff. And the ladies were right. There were a lot of diamonds there. As he sorted through things, he let Nicole know what he was doing.

"Nic, I'm in."

"In what?" Nicole tersely replied, the implication clear.

Bridge laughed. "Uh, the safe. What'd you think I meant I was in?"

"Exactly that." There was still anger in her voice, which her partner found amusing.

"Going through them now."

"I sure hope you mean the safe and not the girls."

Bridge couldn't hide his smile as he examined the contents of the safe. "Of course that's what I meant."

"Don't enjoy this too much, Luke."

"Wouldn't think of it."

"There could be repercussions, you know."

"Nonsense. I've acted completely professional in every sense of the girl, I mean, word. Sorry, slip of the tongue there."

"Enjoying this, are you?"

"I have to admit, a little bit."

It took some time, but Bridge finally got to the end of the stuff. There was one pouch remaining that the diamonds could be in. Bridge emptied the pouch, letting the diamonds fall onto the desk. They weren't Drewiskie's. Bridge sighed in frustration, his disappointment evident to the girls still sitting on the floor, quietly.

"Is it not what you were looking for?" the naked woman asked.

He looked at her and shook his head. "It is not."

"You're not going to take what's there?" the woman in red asked.

"I told you, I was only here for one thing. I'm not interested in anything else."

The naked woman leaned back and stuck her chest out, hoping she could finally interest him in something else. "Nothing?"

"Umm..." Bridge didn't finish his thought and instead let Nicole know. "It's not here, Nic. The diamonds aren't here."

"Did you look anywhere else?"

"No. They said everything was in this safe."

"Ever think maybe they're lying?"

Bridge then looked at the naked woman. "They don't look like the type that would do that."

"Oh really? They're Machado's... women. You really think they're going to tell you everything?"

Bridge then took his eyes off the woman, not wanting to stare at her too much and encourage her thoughts.

"I'll keep looking." Bridge then turned to the red bikini woman. "Is there anywhere else that he might be keeping diamonds?"

The woman thought for a few seconds, then shook

her head. "Not that I'm aware of. If he does, it's not known to me."

"How long have you all been... with him?"

"All of us have been around him at least a year, except for Inez. She's only been here a couple of months."

"Can I just ask a question? What are you all doing with him? Is he that nice a guy?"

"He treats us well, if that's what you're asking. He gives us money, jewelry, freedom of the house. And we can come and go as we please. If you're wondering if we know what he does, we do, but that doesn't concern us. We're not involved in any of that. He does his business when we're not around or if someone comes, he sends us to the pool."

"Nice gig."

"All that he asks from us is our loyalty."

"So you never dime him out?" Bridge asked.

"Not to anyone. Except now."

"Relax. He never needs to know you showed me up here. Besides, I would have found it, anyway. You just made it faster."

"Thank you."

"So none of you know another spot where these diamonds would be? You've never seen them? He supposedly got them from a guy in New York. Possibly Los Angeles."

The woman thought for a few moments. "I remember him saying something about having his eyes on some diamonds that were in New York, I believe. This was maybe eight or nine months ago."

"Did he say whether he got them?"

"I don't remember him talking about it after that. He only said that he wasn't successful in his attempt to get these diamonds."

"Was he happy, sad, what?"

"He didn't seem all that upset about it. He laughed about it and moved on. That's all he said."

"Well, I have to keep looking throughout the house to see if he hid these somewhere else."

"We understand. Are you going to put us to sleep now?"

"No. You've all been very cooperative, and I thank you for that. Can I trust you to be quiet and not call Machado about me being here while I look?"

The women all looked at each other and nodded. "You have our word."

"On one condition," the naked woman interrupted.

Bridge closed his eyes, wondering what was about to come. "Which is?"

"You make sure you see me before you leave."

"You never give up, do you?"

The woman tilted her head and looked at him lustily. "I always get what I want."

The woman in the red bikini smiled at Bridge. "She does, too."

"Well, we'll just have to see about that," Bridge replied.

14

Bridge was looking through some of the other rooms and had only gotten about five minutes into his search when Nicole boomed into his ear with some unsettling news.

"Uh, Luke, we got a problem."

"What?"

"You've got company."

"They're in a completely different room now, Nic. I think the joke's gone on long enough."

"I'm not talking about the girls."

"Then what?"

"Backups just arrived."

"Well, that's what you're out there for, isn't it?"

"Umm, there's about twelve of them."

"Oh."

"They're going in now. Get out of there!"

Bridge decided his partner was right. The

diamonds weren't there, and all he needed to worry about now was getting out of there with his life intact. He ran out of the room he was in and sprinted down the hallway. The naked woman exited the room she was in at the same time, just by coincidence, and stood in front of Bridge to prevent him from going.

"Not getting away from me that fast," she said, throwing her arms around his neck.

"This is all very nice, but I really do have to go."

The woman shook her head. "The only place you're going is my bed."

Bridge laughed uncomfortably, about the situation, about her breasts digging into his chest, about it all. "Uh, we're about to have company here, and I really do have to go."

Bridge slid down a little, pulling the woman's arms off him. Then he slipped past her and continued running.

"Sorry, you're really nice and all!" Bridge's voice faded as he ran down the stairs. As he ran through the living room, he saw the rest of the ladies sitting on the couch. "Bye, girls, thanks for everything!"

He ran past the women, who watched him as he sprinted to the back door, wondering what the issue was. Bridge continued running, going through the door, and by the pool. Just as he got past the pool, he saw a few men coming up by the sand near the grass.

"Uh oh."

Bridge turned around, but didn't see much. As

soon as he did, he felt something hard and heavy strike him along the top of the head. His body fell back, plunging into the pool. He floated unconscious near the top for a few moments.

"Get in there and get him before he drowns," a man said.

Bridge was pulled out of the pool, then carried into the house. As he was carried into a room on the first floor, the leader of the group stopped to question the ladies about what had happened. The naked woman had come down the stairs, with clothes on now, though still not much, while the others explained what had happened. They told the truth as they knew it, all except the part when they told Bridge where the safe was. But they said the stranger treated them well, and that he was looking for diamonds. That was all they knew.

"Luke, are you out of there?" Nicole asked.

She tried asking the same question several more times for a few more minutes. After getting no response, she knew what that meant. Now, she was going to have to go to work. She got out and went to her trunk, opening it, looking through her bag to make sure she had everything she needed. She'd give it another twenty minutes, in the event that Bridge wasn't captured yet but was hiding and remaining radio silent in case the men were nearby. She knew that was unlikely, but it had happened before. That's why she was giving him twenty minutes. It was enough time for him to get out of the situation, and if he was already captured, it was still a short enough time that she could get in there and extract him. That was the general rule they always agreed upon if they were separated and lost contact with each other. Wait twenty minutes, see if the situation has changed, and if not, then barge in.

As she sat in her car and waited, about ten minutes had elapsed. She was getting restless and was about to make her move. She wasn't the most patient, especially when Bridge's life was at stake. Nicole was about to get out and do her thing, when she suddenly stopped, hearing a loud noise, and it was getting louder by the second. She knew what that noise was. She looked up at the sky and saw a helicopter approaching the house, eventually hovering over top of Machado's property. It was the same chopper that Machado had left in earlier. Eventually, she lost sight of it as it descended on the helipad in the back of the house.

Nicole leaned her head back on the headrest, closed her eyes, shook her head, and sighed. She knew she was walking into a hornet's nest now. As hard as it was going to be before, she knew security was going to be amped up even more. She waited a few more minutes, going over the plan in her mind, making sure she had everything covered.

While she was still debating it, Machado was led into the house, and then into the room where they had Bridge secured. Bridge was sitting in a chair, his arms tied behind him, strapped to the chair, though he still wasn't awake yet. His head slumped forward as he slept. Once Machado was given all the details that they knew up to that point, he motioned to one of his men to wake Bridge up. Someone had grabbed a bucket of water, then splashed it in Bridge's face, his eyes immediately popping open. He coughed a couple of times, then his eyes strained to figure out what was going on. Machado gave him a minute or two to clear his head before asking any questions. And there would be a lot of questions.

"Hello there," Machado said, smiling from ear to ear, trying to be friendly, as if no one had broken into his house and knocked out his guards.

"Hi," Bridge replied.

"Perhaps you could tell me what you are doing here in my house?"

"Oh, is this your house? I'm so sorry. You know what it was? I was swimming along the shore, then I saw this girl out there on the beach. She had a white bikini on, you know? So, you know, one thing led to another, so I kind of followed her in, then I saw all these other fine-looking ladies, and—"

Machado was already tired of the lie. "So you decided to put tranquilizer darts in her. As well as the rest of my men?"

"Well, they thought I had bad intentions or something. Understandable, I suppose, but you know how it is."

"No, I don't know how it is. Who just carries around tranquilizer darts with them?"

"Um, someone who... has gotten mugged before?"

"Then you carry a gun. With real bullets. And not while you're swimming."

"I'm kind of strange, I guess."

"You better start telling me the truth or you'll be kind of dead... I guess."

"Uh, yeah, sure, I could do that, but before I do, you think you could untie me from this chair. It really chafes my wrists and all."

"No."

"You know, why do you guys always tie people to chairs? I mean, this isn't the first time I've been like this, you know."

"It doesn't surprise me."

"You guys really need to figure out some alternative methods."

"We could just leave you tied up and stuff you in a barrel, then drop you in the ocean. Would that suffice as different enough?"

"Uh, yeah. I don't like that nearly as much as this though," Bridge said.

"Maybe you could stop with the fun and games and tell me what you're really doing here. If you do, and I think it's reasonable, you might just leave here with your legs still attached to your body. If not, you might not ever leave this room alive."

"OK, you're gonna think this is really crazy."

Machado put his hand up. "Save the lies." He turned to his top aide. "Show this man what happens when people lie to us."

"Oh no," Bridge said, knowing what that meant.

Several of the men moved in on Bridge, who dejectedly tried to brace himself for what he knew was coming. The sound of flesh being hit by scarred up knuckles was soon heard, Bridge's face being used as a punching bag. Several of the men had red knuckles from the blood that splattered on them from Bridge's face, who now had several prime cuts on it. After a few minutes, when they thought his face had had enough, they moved on to Bridge's midsection, pummeling him with rights and lefts from multiple hands. After a few more minutes, they stopped their assault on Bridge's body. Machado called his dogs off and they backed away, allowing their leader to move in closer. He was now standing only a foot away from Bridge.

"Have you had enough?"

Bridge swished some blood around in his mouth and spit it out to the side. He thought about spitting at Machado's face, but he really did have enough of the beating, and that would likely only cause more of a problem. So he thought he'd be nice and just spit on the floor.

"Uh, yeah, I'd say so," Bridge said.

"Now, would you like to tell me what it is you're really doing here? The truth?"

"The truth? You really want the truth?"

"Yes, but before you begin, let me explain to you that I'm not a very patient man. And I don't have the tolerance to play these games much longer. If you do not tell me what it is that I want to know, right now, you will be taken down to the beach and you will be shot. Then we will throw your body in the ocean for the sharks."

"Dead bodies in the ocean have a way of turning up."

"Not if we attach some raw meat to your body to make it more appealing for the sharks to eat you up."

It wasn't a very appealing proposition for Bridge, who shuddered at the thought. "Do you think I could get some aspirin? My head's killing me."

"You tell me what I want to know or there will be something else killing you."

"And if I tell you?"

"If it is nothing so severe, maybe I'll laugh about it, and we all go our separate ways. No harm done."

"And if it is severe?"

"Then we will cross that bridge when we come to it."

Bridge sighed, figuring he might as well spill it. Maybe he would learn something in the process. Something that would tell him where the diamonds really were. He just had to hope that Nicole was out there somewhere, close to getting in. Right now, he had to keep Machado talking, and himself alive, long enough for Nicole to get to him.

"OK. So here's the deal," Bridge said. "I was hired by a man named Stephen Drewiskie. He had his diamonds stolen a few months ago, and I was hired to find them."

Machado started laughing. "And you think I have them?"

"Well, it's not what I think. It's what he thinks."

Machado continued laughing. "This is preposterous."

"What? You're saying you didn't take them?"

"What do you think I am? A common thief?"

Bridge tried to shrug, though it was difficult to do so with his arms restrained like they were. "Well..."

"So that's what you broke in here for? His diamonds?"

"That's it. I promise I wasn't taking anything else. You can even check."

"I already have. You broke into my safe."

"Yeah, sorry about that. Hazard of the job."

"I would have thought that the condition of the last two people Mr. Drewiskie sent to me looking for his diamonds... I would have thought he would have gotten the message."

"Apparently he did not."

"So it seems. I thought I made it perfectly clear I did not take his diamonds. I guess I have to make a bigger statement."

"Just for the record, if you didn't take them, do you know who did?"

"I do not."

"But you were interested in them."

"Yes. Who wouldn't be? They were magnificent. Worth a fortune."

"But you didn't offer him a fortune," Bridge said.

"I made an offer on a whim, hoping that he needed money desperately enough to sell them on the cheap. He didn't. I moved on. It's as simple as that."

"Oh. OK. Well, I'll be sure enough to tell him when I get back to the States."

"One more thing we have to talk about."

"Oh? What's that?"

"You don't happen to know anything about my home in Los Angeles being broken into recently, do you?"

"Me? No. Haven't been to L.A. in over two years now. I'm an east coast man myself. Hate the hot weather out west. How do you like it?"

"It's nice. Very enjoyable. Except for when people break into my home when I'm not there and get into my safe. Like what happened here."

"Hmm. Interesting. Maybe Drewiskie hired someone else to look out there."

"Or perhaps it was you."

"Uh, no, already told you, haven't been there in years. Wasn't me."

"I think maybe it was."

"Oh. Well, I give you my word, you'll never see me

again, and I'll tell Drewiskie you definitely didn't take the diamonds."

"I would appreciate that. But I think maybe I'll tell him myself."

"Oh. Great. I'll just go on my merry way then if your people will untie me."

Machado smiled. "I think that is more complicated than it seems."

"What's complicated? Just untie these ropes here, I'll walk out whatever door you want me to, and I'm on the first plane out of here."

"I think maybe you need to be made an example of."

Bridge laughed, hoping to diffuse the situation. "You've already done that. Believe me, this face isn't gonna heal for weeks. Months, maybe. And if you want me to tell people where I got it, I will be more than happy to spread the word."

"I think we'll have to spread something else. Like your body all over the sand."

"That doesn't sound very appealing. Whatever happened to letting me go?"

"I have changed my mind about that."

"You said if I was honest. I was."

"And I thank you for that. But how would it look if I just let go of a man who broke into my home, knocked out my guards, and steal my women?"

"Uh, to be clear, I was not stealing any of your

women. Not one. And I was a perfect gentleman around them at all times. You can ask them."

"Be that as it may, if I let you go, it sets a bad example for others. Then every idiot with half a brain will think that he can just waltz in here whenever he feels like it and take from me without any repercussions. I'm afraid I can't have that."

"How 'bout this?" Bridge asked, trying to think of anything to stall. "What if you let me go? And I promise I won't tell anyone I was ever here."

Machado smiled. "I think I do not trust you."

"What if we make another kind of deal? I have money."

Machado stopped walking away and looked at him. "Money?"

"Yes. A lot of it. And it's yours if you let me go."

"How much?"

"Uh, let's see… have to add up all the different bank accounts I have. Let's see… two, three, five hundred, one, two… about five million."

Machado raised his eyebrows, impressed by the amount. "Five million?"

"Yes. And it's yours if you let me go."

"And just how would we arrange this transaction?"

"Umm, I dunno. You could have a couple of your goon—fine associates come with me to a bank where I can do a money transfer into your accounts?"

"It is a very interesting proposition," Machado said.

"So what do you say? Do we have a deal?"

"Unfortunately for you, money is not one of my problems. I've got all the money I need. Five million does nothing for me."

"What kind of answer is that? Five million does nothing for me. Five million is five million. That's enough for anybody."

"Except for me when someone breaks into my home. I'm afraid there's only one solution. You'll be taken down to the beach and taken care of."

"What if I work for you instead?" Bridge asked.

"Work for me?"

"Hey, you could probably use someone with my skills working for you. I mean, if I could get in here, maybe you have enemies that you would like to turn the tables on?"

Machado folded his arms and put his hand on his chin, apparently thinking, looking like he was actually considering the proposal. "That is an interesting proposition."

"I can break in just about anywhere, I can open a safe, I can handle a gun, what do you say?"

Machado looked at one of his aides, seriously pondering the question. His aide just shrugged, not sure himself. "And how would I know I could trust you to remain loyal? That you wouldn't just take off at the first point you were left alone?"

"Uh, I dunno. You got one of those ankle monitors or something? App on my phone? I dunno, whatever."

"That is a very tempting offer. I probably could use

someone like you in my organization. But I think I will just kill you instead."

Bridge blew air through his mouth, hoping his partner would get there in time before Machado made an example out of him.

"Take him down to the beach and kill him. Then chop him up into small pieces and feed him to the sharks."

Bridge shook his head as he listened to their plans for him. "Not. Appealing. At all."

15

Bridge was untied and lifted up from his chair with the help of three of Machado's guards. He could try to resist and fight whoever was nearby, but it would have been futile seeing six men in there against him. And they were all bigger than he was. His best bet was still Nicole. And he prayed that whatever she was planning, it was happening soon.

"Get him out of here," Machado said.

"Pleasure doing business with you," Bridge said, smiling as he left the room.

"Pleasure was all mine."

Bridge was paraded through the living room, the girls now missing from the couch. Everyone then stopped, the house suddenly starting to shake from an explosion on the grounds outside the back of the house. There was another explosion. Everyone dropped to the ground, including Bridge.

"What's going on?" one of the men asked.

"I think we're under attack," another one said.

Machado came running out of the room to see what was happening, but he was quickly knocked off his feet from another explosion in front of the house. Machado got to his knees, then started directing his men on where to go. It was obvious they were under attack, and they couldn't just sit still and wait for the whole house to blow up. Before any of his men were able to move, though, Nicole suddenly appeared from the stairs, ripping off dozens of rounds from her assault rifle, all the bullets finding a permanent residence in the wall. A few paintings fell off the wall, with some newfound holes in it, and a TV was destroyed, but it served its purpose of getting everyone's attention.

"Everyone drop your weapons, nice and slow," Nicole said. "Or else that wall won't be the only thing that's got holes in it." A few of the men were slow to comply with her wishes, thinking she couldn't possibly get all of them, or that she wouldn't actually do what she said. "If you're thinking I won't plug you, you're sadly mistaken."

One of the men obviously didn't believe her and went for his gun. He wasn't even able to get it out of its holster. Nicole shot him several times, then pointed her rifle back at the rest of the men.

"Anybody else wanna try me?"

The men immediately dropped their guns. This woman meant business.

"And untie him."

Bridge was untied, and he scurried over to Nicole's position, standing next to her. She handed Bridge her rifle, then took the extra one off her shoulder. Another explosion rocked the house, water from the pool saturating the back windows.

"We should be going," Nicole said. "The others out there are going to keep blowing things up until we're safely on our way."

"This isn't over," Machado replied.

Bridge rolled his eyes at the threat. "C'mon, we both got in our shots, it's over now. I broke in, you beat me up, we're even."

"I'll find out who you are."

"Listen, Hector, the only thing I'm interested in with you was those diamonds, and if you said you didn't take them, then we're done here."

"You think so?"

"Come on, stop trying to be a badass and just listen to reason," Bridge said. "If you wanna continue a war, we can, but you already know I can break into every residence you have. You got your pride hurt, I got some cuts and bruises. Let's just call it a day, huh?"

"We'll see."

"Great. Uh, one more thing: if you didn't take the diamonds, do you know who did?"

"I already told you. I don't know."

"Oh. I wasn't sure if you were being honest or not. I

thought the whole gun thing pointed at you would change your tune. Guess not."

"Let's go," Nicole said, uncomfortable standing there for too long.

Another explosion went off, again near the back of the house.

"Just go and stop blowing my property apart!" Machado yelled.

"We're going," Bridge said.

"Word of warning," Nicole said. "First person who comes out after us is going to get a bullet in their head."

Bridge and Nicole ran over to the door, keeping their eyes on the men in case they did something foolish. Nobody was that stupid, though. Bridge and Nicole quickly exited the house through the front door, then ran down the street until they got to their car. They jumped into it as fast as they could ever remember getting into one, then Nicole put the car in reverse, smoke rising into the air from the pressure on the tires. After reversing for a few seconds, she spun the car around, speeding away from the house, hoping no one would be following them, though they kind of expected that someone would. Much to their surprise, and happiness, it didn't appear that anyone did.

"Where to?" Nicole asked.

"Let's get back to the hotel and pack our bags and get out of here."

"Already did. In the back seat."

Bridge looked back and saw their luggage, not that they ever travelled with much. They learned to pack light over the years, the product of having to move quickly at times.

"When'd you do that?" Bridge asked.

"While you were still getting ready and going over plans at the hotel. I told you I was putting stuff away."

"Guess I wasn't listening."

"It's about time you admitted it. Airport?"

Bridge nodded. "Airport." He looked in the mirror. "Doesn't look like they're following now, but that doesn't mean they're not gonna try. The sooner we get out of here the better."

As soon as they got back to the airport, Bridge immediately booked tickets for Miami. It was a flight that left in two hours. As they waited in the lounge, they kept a lookout for any of Machado's men showing up.

"Why Miami?" Nicole asked. "Does Machado have some type of secret residence there too that I don't know about?"

Bridge shook his head, finally sitting down after pacing for the last several minutes.

"Look, I don't know if Machado's going to really come after us or not. Or at least try to. But if he does, then I would say it's possible, probably even likely, that he's got contacts working here somewhere. And if he does come looking for us, if we fly straight to New York, it's a good assumption he'll think that's where we live."

"But if we fly to Miami, he'll think that's our home base," Nicole said, understanding his reasoning.

"Exactly. Now, if he wants to spend the next few months roaming around Miami looking for us, more power to him."

"So how long are we going to stay there?"

"As long as it takes for us to get another flight out of there. I figure if we fly to Miami first, there should be another flight to New York sometime soon after we get there."

Nicole was good with the plan. But her mind then wandered back to Machado and the diamonds.

"What do you think about Machado? About what he said?"

"About not taking the diamonds?" Bridge asked, getting a confirmation from his girlfriend. "I don't know."

"He sounded sincere. Maybe he was lying, I don't know."

Bridge's eyes darted around the floor as he contemplated. "I don't think he is. Before you got there, when he was questioning me, he said the same thing. He made a lowball offer, hoping Drewiskie needed money badly enough to accept it, and when he didn't, he moved on. Those were his exact words."

"And you think he was telling the truth?"

"I do. Strangely enough. I asked those girls if they'd ever seen the diamonds, even showed them a picture of it. They'd never seen them either. And while we were waiting for the safe to open, they said Machado liked to show off his jewelry, even the stuff that didn't get worn."

"Which would indicate that he didn't have it. Or that he was still wary of showing it yet."

Bridge sighed and cleared his throat. "Uh… I don't think so. I really believe he was leveling. I don't think he took them."

"What if he kept them in another room that nobody knows about? I'm sure he's got a secret stash of stuff somewhere. Guys like him always do."

"I guess it's possible. I just didn't get that feeling. I think we're barking up the wrong tree here. We've checked two houses, broken into two safes, almost gotten killed, and the diamonds aren't anywhere, and nobody's admitted to seeing them. I think we're on a wild goose chase here."

"If that's so, then who took them?"

"I don't know."

"We're back to square one," Nicole said.

"Seems that way. You know, before we left, when I talked to Eric, he said this might happen. That we were taking it on blind faith that Machado's the one who actually stole them. I wonder if he knew more than what he was saying."

"I doubt Eric would have let us go after this guy if he knew who took them."

"You're probably right. It was probably just him

warning us to dig more before getting our hooks on someone."

"Probably should've listened."

"Well, you know me, act first, listen second."

"We should also tell our client he's wrong."

Bridge nodded. "Yep. Looks that way."

"You think he deliberately..." Nicole stopped mid-sentence, thinking what she was about to suggest was crazy. "Nah. Never mind."

"What? Just spit it out. I'm sure whatever you were about to say isn't the craziest thing that's ever come out of your mouth."

"Gee, thanks."

"So?"

"I was just gonna say, what if Drewiskie specifically sent us after Machado, knowing he wasn't the real guy?" Nicole said.

"Why would he do that?"

"I don't know. Just spitting things out."

"Wouldn't make sense," Bridge said. "He came to us. We didn't go to him. What, you were thinking he actually has the diamonds, or he knows who really took them?"

"Yeah, something like that. I know, it's crazy."

"Wouldn't be so crazy if we just stumbled onto this. Wouldn't be the first time we were lied to by a client. But if he wanted us out of the way, he wouldn't have hired us to begin with."

"Yeah, you're right. I was just thinking."

"Remember that housekeeper of his? The one I was skeptical of?"

"Yeah?"

"Maybe we should circle back to her again. I always thought from the beginning there was something fishy about her."

"That was just you being…"

"No, seriously, if someone cloned that briefcase, and Drewiskie rarely took it out of the house, who would know it better than her?"

"Um, the proof?"

"We don't need proof," Bridge replied. "We're not the police. We're allowed to go off half-cocked."

"And often do."

"And we're often right. Let's just hope this is one of those times."

"And if we're not?"

"Then we got a long road ahead of us."

16

Just as Bridge said they would, they landed back in New York after a connecting flight from Miami. Bridge was especially concerned about Machado trying to follow them, but they saw no activity that indicated that he actually was. It was a long and tiring journey back from Brazil, so Bridge didn't call Drewiskie until the following morning.

"How's the hunt coming?" Drewiskie asked.

Bridge laughed, thinking of the last few days. "Well, it's been interesting."

"What's that mean? Have you found them yet?"

"There's been some complications."

"Such as?"

"We just got back from Brazil."

"With the diamonds?"

"No. We don't have the diamonds. I did speak with Machado about them, though."

"Spoke to him? Somewhat unusual, isn't it?"

"Well, there were a lot of things happening at the time, guns, bombs, you don't even wanna know all the details."

"What about the diamonds?"

"I've gotten into both of his houses, broken into two of his safes, taken a beating in the process, and the diamonds aren't there."

"So he hid them somewhere?"

"I don't think so," Bridge answered. "I don't think he has them."

"What do you mean he doesn't have them? Of course he has them. He's the only one who could have them. Who else would it be?"

"He's not the only one. He was just the most likely. I think we can safely rule him out."

"Are you positive about that?"

"I'm in the ninety-five percent range on that one."

Drewiskie sighed. He thought for sure Machado had them. "Who else could it be then?"

"I think we're back to where we were at the beginning. Someone on the list of people that knows you."

"It's... hard to believe that."

"Well, right now, it's one of three people. It's either Machado, in which case if he's got them, he's hiding them extremely well, and I'm not sure I'll be able to get them. Or it could be someone on your list, in which case we have to do more digging. And third, it could be someone else completely that we don't know about, and if that's the case, we can probably pack it up and go home now because there's no way we'll be able to find them without leaving clues behind. So right now, your best bet, and what you should be hoping for, is that it is someone on that list."

"I hear what you're saying."

"Are you still in New York?"

"No, I'm back in Los Angeles now," Drewiskie said.

"OK, good. I'm thinking about going back there, having another look at your house."

"Yeah, I'm here, just give me a few hours' notice before you get here so I can fit my appointments around you."

"You don't have to do anything different to accommodate us. We can work it just like last time if you want. If your housekeeper's there, she can show us in so we don't inconvenience you."

"Oh, well, she's not here right now, so I'll have to make arrangements for you."

"What do you mean she's not there? Where is she?"

"She called me a couple days ago, said she had a family emergency, her sister was in the hospital or something, so she asked if she could go see her."

"Where?" Bridge asked.

"Boston I believe it was."

"Boston, huh?"

"Something wrong?"

"Uh, I don't know. I'll get back to you."

Bridge put his phone down and stared at the wall. Nicole came out of the bedroom and saw her boyfriend zoning out, immediately recognizing the look.

"What's wrong?"

Bridge turned to look at her. "I just talked to Drewiskie."

"He wasn't happy about Machado? Still believes it was him?"

"No, it's not that. He's back in Los Angeles."

"So? He lives there, you know."

"It's the housekeeper, Denise Ragland. She left on an emergency."

"So what's the problem?"

"You don't think that's strange?" Bridge asked. "I mean, she just happens to have an emergency a couple days after we talk to her, which conveniently gets her out of the city?"

"Where'd she go?"

"He said Boston."

"Should be easy enough to check."

"You didn't check backgrounds on anybody on the list, did you?"

"No, just checked financial statements mostly." Nicole stared at him for a second. "You don't think she has a sister, do you? I can tell by your face."

"I dunno. Maybe she has a sister. I have my doubts about whether there was an emergency, though."

MIKE RYAN

Nicole immediately went over to her computer and typed in Ragland's name. Everything they needed about her background came back within a few minutes. After Nicole read her file, she looked at her partner. Now it was Bridge's turn to recognize the look. She had that face that indicated she found out something interesting.

"You ready?"

"Give it to me," Bridge replied.

"Well, Denise Ragland does indeed have a sister. But she doesn't live in Boston."

"Where does she live?"

"A cemetery. She died about twenty years ago."

"Maybe she has another sister? Brother?"

"Looks like there were two children. Two girls."

"What about parents?"

"Parents are also deceased."

"So what you're telling me is that she's the only surviving member of her family?"

"That's the size of it."

"Husband, kids, pets, anything like that? Cousins?"

"No, no, no, and no. Married, divorced, no kids, no family that she's close to that I can tell."

"Boyfriend?"

Nicole shrugged, her hands landing firmly down on the desk. "I dunno, I mean, not that I can tell, unless it's pretty recent."

Bridge popped a piece of gum into his mouth and started chewing. "We need to get into her phone records. Find out who she's been talking to, especially after we visited. That should tell us something."

"Already working on it."

Another hour went by before Nicole finally had the information they were looking for. She printed out a list of numbers, then started cross-referencing some of them.

"We got her," Nicole blurted out, tossing her pen down on the desk.

"We do?"

"Well, not physically, but I mean, it's her. It's gotta be."

"I've been telling you that for ages, but you wouldn't listen. What's changing your mind now?"

"She called the same number twelve times in three days after we visited Los Angeles."

"And? What's that mean? Whose number was it?"

Nicole pulled up a picture on the computer. "This guy. His name is Christopher McClendon."

"Don't mean nothing to me. Who's he?"

"For one, he's a convicted felon. Served several terms in prison for armed robbery."

"Oh, nice. What are they, a couple?"

"Could be. His number appears in her records every day for the past year."

"Maybe this guy put her up to it," Bridge said. "He starts wining and dining, schmoozing her over with the intention of having her help him lift Drewiskie's diamonds."

"Or maybe she recruited him. She got tired of working for him, didn't like how she was treated, her pay, whatever, and decided she was gonna work for herself. She somehow got connected to this guy, and now they're in it together."

"Well, whatever the case, whoever recruited who, it seems like they're now connected, doesn't it?"

"Seems that way."

"What about other numbers?" Bridge asked.

"Nothing that appears as often as McClendon's. And it's not even close."

"So if we're moving on from Machado, it sounds like these two are our best option right now."

"It would appear so."

"Where's McClendon located?"

"You ready for this?"

"Why do you keep asking me that? Of course I'm ready. Just tell me."

"Los Angeles."

"Los Angeles? What, they didn't go anywhere?"

"I'm digging into her records now," Nicole said. "She's made no major purchases on her credit card, no plane tickets or anything like that, she hasn't gone anywhere. And McClendon's calls are coming from L.A."

"Well, guess we're going back to the City of Angels."

"Why do they call it that, anyway?"

Bridge shrugged. "I don't know. Never really thought about it before."

"I mean, if that's the City of Angels, I'd hate to see what the alternative is. Because I don't really see a lot of angel-like behavior there."

"Well, one thing's for sure, there isn't gonna be much when we get there either."

17

Once Bridge and Nicole arrived in L.A., they checked in with Drewiskie to see if he had any information for them. He had tried to get in touch with Ragland while Bridge and Nicole were on the flight out there. He had no luck, however. His housekeeper wasn't returning his calls or messages. Bridge and Nicole first went to the only address that they had on McClendon, which was an apartment on the east side. It was a third-floor apartment, so staking it out was going to be tough. And they could be wasting a lot of time they didn't have if he wasn't there. So instead of waiting, Bridge figured he'd do the next best thing. He'd just knock on the door and see if someone answered.

"Don't you think that's a little risky?" Nicole asked.

"Not unless he shoots through the door."

"And what if he does that?"

"Then I guess it's risky."

"Maybe we should just wait here in the parking for a while first?"

"McClendon doesn't have a car registered in his name, and Ragland's car isn't here. I suspect McClendon doesn't have one at all, legally that is, so we wouldn't know what that car is, anyway. And waiting for one of them to appear could take days if they decided to hole themselves up in there. And if they decided to fly the coop, we'll be sitting here giving them additional time to float away."

"We got one thing going for us though."

"What's that?"

"They apparently haven't sold the diamonds. I think we'd have heard some chatter if they did."

"Not necessarily," Bridge said. "If they sold them to somebody like Machado, you think any of them are going to broadcast it?"

"Yeah, probably not."

"Let me just knock on the door and see what happens. If I hear something, we know they're there. If I don't, we know to keep looking. But I don't wanna just sit here and not know either way."

"And if someone answers? What are you going to say? I don't see any encyclopedias in your hand."

"I'll think of something."

"I should at least go in as backup," Nicole said.

"No, just stay here, keep a lookout, keep your eyes on the door, make sure nobody comes in that I need to worry about."

Bridge got out of the car and went up to the address on file for McClendon. As he walked down the third-floor hallway, he passed a few rough-looking characters, as one would expect to find in that neighborhood. Once he got to the room he was looking for, Bridge stepped to the side of it and knocked. Like many police officers, he also didn't like standing in front of closed doors without knowing what was on the other side of it. Especially when it was someone like McClendon, who could have been easily holding a shotgun or rifle on the other side and decide to start blasting away. Luckily it didn't come to that. But on the other hand, it didn't come to anything. Nobody answered the door. And though Bridge leaned over and put his ear against the door, he couldn't hear anything inside. No voices, radio, television, footsteps moving, trying to be quiet. Nothing. He knocked for a few more minutes, hoping something would present itself. Nothing did. Instead of giving up and going back to the car, Bridge started knocking on some doors, hoping one of McClendon's neighbors would know something about him or where he went.

While Bridge was inside, Nicole figured she'd get some more help in fixing their problem. She called Eric Happ again, hoping he would be able to do just that. Thankfully, he answered on the second ring.

"Hey stranger," Happ said.

"Hey. How's things?"

"Pretty good. What are you up to?"

"Uh, I need a favor."

"Of course you do. You know, you're getting to be just as bad as Luke."

"Is that an insult?"

"It was meant to be."

"Well, I'll overlook it this time."

"Thanks so much. What do you need?"

Nicole told him everything they'd been up to at that point, including going down to Brazil, coming back, and what led them back to Los Angeles.

"You know, I told Luke before you guys started all this not to assume that Machado took them. He didn't listen."

"He never does," Nicole said. "But what about this McClendon guy? You think you can help?"

"I guess I can try."

"There's nothing in my records about aliases, but maybe you've got better sources than I do."

"Well, that's a given."

"Or maybe you can check and see if you've heard anything about the diamonds. Whether they're on the market, already sold, left the country, whatever."

"Am I getting paid for this?" Happ asked.

"Uh, I can give you a hug next time I see you."

"Throw in a kiss on the cheek, and you got a deal."

"Done!"

"OK, I'll start checking around with some people and see if they've heard anything. I'll get back to you on it."

"Thanks, Eric, you're a lifesaver."

"Uh huh."

A few minutes later, Nicole saw her partner leave the apartment building. He was walking normally, she didn't see any blood on him, and there didn't seem to be any holes in his body. Everything must have gone according to his plan. He didn't seem that happy, though. Of course, he often looked that way. Once Bridge got back in the car, he sat there, looking through the windshield. Nicole turned to look at him.

"Came up empty, huh?"

"Yeah, nobody's there," Bridge replied.

"Well, that doesn't mean they're not there for good. Maybe they went to the store or something?"

"No, they're gone. I talked to one of the neighbors who lives across the hall. Said she saw McClendon and a woman leave yesterday. Had a bunch of suitcases and stuff with them."

"A woman? Ragland?"

Bridge shook his head. "Not the woman she described. She said this girl was younger, late twenties, early thirties, black hair, average figure."

"Maybe McClendon's girlfriend."

"Could be."

"So how does Ragland fit in then?"

"This neighbor has seen Ragland there," Bridge answered. "I described her, and she said she's seen a woman there matching that description."

"So what's that tell us?"

"That Ragland is probably not involved with McClendon romantically. Most likely a pure business relationship. One recruited the other, Ragland as the inside source, telling McClendon when the best time to hit would be, him pulling off the job, then all getting a split of the money once it's sold."

"This neighbor didn't happen to know where they were going, did she?"

"No, McClendon didn't talk much. He'd only been living there a few months, apparently."

"So where's that leave us?"

Bridge leaned back in his seat and thought, putting his hand up to his mouth. "I don't know. We don't know who this girlfriend is. We don't know where McClendon's going, and we don't know where Ragland is either."

"I can try to get into McClendon's financial accounts, bank, credit cards, see if he made any purchases like airline tickets."

"Yeah, I have a feeling he wouldn't do that. At least not him personally. He's been in the joint a few times, knows how things work. At least I would assume. He knows that type of stuff can be tracked, traced. I don't think he's dumb enough to do it on his accounts."

"The girlfriend."

Bridge nodded. "The girlfriend. Can't hack into someone's accounts if you don't know who they are. And if that woman doesn't have a criminal record?

Forget about it. By the time we find out who she is, we won't need the information anymore."

"While you were in there, I called Happ. He's looking into it now. Maybe he'll be able to get something for us."

"Maybe. Can't really count on that though."

"Didn't say we were counting on it. Just said maybe he can help."

"Can he help in time though?"

Nicole shrugged. "Why not? As far as I know, there's no time limit on this thing."

"Not officially anyway. But you know as well as I do, if they've still got the diamonds, it'll go much easier for us if we can track them down before they sell them. Because if we can't, and they do wind up selling them, finding out who the person is that bought them is going to be a monumental effort. And one that won't come easily. Our best bet is finding them before they unload the diamonds."

"I don't understand why they haven't sold them yet. What are they waiting for?"

"Probably for the heat to die down. They stole them, what, three, four months ago? Something like that?"

"Yeah."

"So you're not going to unload them right away. There's too much heat, pressure. Cops are involved, looking at everybody, then you got insurance investigators. So you lie low for a little bit, wait for it to die down."

"Makes sense."

"But then, just when it starts to die down, then Drewiskie hires a couple people to keep on looking. The search continues, which means the heat's still on. You gotta play it cool, not panic."

"Then we come along..."

"And the heat's still on, we're in town, we're looking for things, still can't make a move yet. But then, we leave town, we go to Brazil for a week, now's their chance. They've got a small window to get ahead of things and make their move, because it might be the best chance they get."

"You're assuming one thing in all of this."

"What's that?" Bridge asked.

"That they actually want to sell the diamonds. Ever occur to you that they might just plan on keeping them for themselves?"

"It did. I dismissed it though."

"Why?"

"What would they want them for? What good are diamonds, and five million dollars worth at that, if you can't show them off? What's the purpose?"

"Unless they're saving them for their retirement fund."

"And what if you never live to see that retirement fund?"

"Then it was for nothing?" Nicole replied.

MIKE RYAN

"Exactly. So there's really no point in that either. Especially Ragland. She knows that. Her sister, her parents, all gone. She knows life can be taken away from you like that." Bridge snapped his fingers to illustrate the point. "No, she wouldn't save for later. She knows that day might not ever come. And McClendon too, for that matter. What good is saving for later when you're a guy with his record? He works and hustles for a living. He also knows there might not be that savings for later. Men like him, they want their money now."

"So where does that leave us?"

"Leaves us with three questions," Bridge said. "We need to find out one of three things. All of them would be preferable, but at least one would get us to where we need to go."

"And they are?"

"Where they're at, where they're going, and who's buying. Those are the three."

"And where do you think we're gonna find the answers?"

"Not sitting in here, that's for sure."

"Back to the hotel?"

Bridge contemplated for a few seconds, then thought he had a better solution. "Let's go back to Drewiskie's place."

"What for?"

"Ragland had her own room there, right?"

"Yeah."

"Maybe there's something in there that will lead us in the direction we need to go."

"I doubt she'd leave a clue behind about anything."

"Why? She's not a career criminal. Doesn't do this for a living. She's not used to, nor is she proficient in covering her tracks. At least she shouldn't be. She's got no training in this sort of thing. The chances of her not making a mistake aren't good. We, on the other hand, are pros. We're supposed to be good at finding the mistakes that people like her make."

"Assuming she made one."

"Yeah," Bridge said. "Assuming she made one."

18

Bridge and Nicole arrived at the Drewiskie residence and were greeted at the front door by the millionaire. Once inside the house, they were immediately taken to Ragland's room, which was located on the first floor, just off the garage.

"I know you said you had evidence that implicated Denise, but I just can't believe it," Drewiskie said. "She's been with me over ten years."

"Well, it's like I said," Bridge replied. "She's got a convicted felon that she's been contacting regularly for a long time, then she vanishes after we talk to her, and she doesn't have a sister in Boston, or any relatives in Boston for that matter."

Drewiskie shook his head and sighed, having a hard time accepting it all. "Still... it's just..."

"I know. It's hard to think someone you've trusted for ten years would turn on you and set you up like that, but it happens. And believe me, you wouldn't be the first."

"So was this her plan from the beginning? From when I first hired her?"

"I would doubt it. Ten years is a long time to set up a score. It's been known to happen, but it's usually by professionals. I would imagine that she just lost her way at some point over the years. Maybe she thought she should've been making more money, maybe she thought you didn't treat her well enough, or maybe she thought she should be somewhere else at that point in her life. Whatever the reason, it's probably been building up, then she acted on it."

"I should've known. I should've seen the signs."

"Some people hide things well," Bridge said. "Wouldn't beat yourself up over it."

Once they arrived at Ragland's room, Bridge and Nicole went to work, looking at, under, or inside everything they came across.

"What exactly are you looking for?" Drewiskie asked.

"I don't know," Bridge answered. "It's one of those deals you know when you find it."

Ragland's room was a fairly big room, measuring over two hundred square feet. It was big enough for a bed, a desk, a refrigerator, and a couch. And it looked pretty comfortable. It wasn't like she was crammed into a small space. Bridge started with the closet, while Nicole began with the desk. They each ripped the place apart, metaphorically speaking, since they weren't actually making a mess. They had both learned over the years how to search through a space without making it look like they were ever there. Throwing books, papers, and other possessions on the floor was an amateurish move, allowing your target to know that someone had been there, and possibly spook them. But doing it in a way that was neat and tidy, clean, and the element of surprise would still be on your side. In this case, it probably wasn't necessary, since they doubted Ragland would ever return, but it was the preferred way they liked to work now.

Once they were done with their respective parts of the room, each moved on. Bridge checked the bed, and underneath it, while Nicole went over to the dresser.

"Anything yet?" Bridge asked.

"Nada," Nicole answered.

"How sure are you that something's here?" Drewiskie asked, impressed with how thoroughly the two of them were covering the room.

"I'm not," Bridge replied. "It just strikes me that she left in a hurry. She's not a professional, just seems like she'd make a mistake and leave something behind. Forget about something. Something like that."

After a quick few minutes, Bridge and Nicole then moved over to a bookshelf almost simultaneously. It was a brown, five shelf bookcase, about thirty-six inches wide, and it was packed with books. They first studied the titles, seeing if there was something interesting about them, a pattern, names of places, but there was none. Then they started going through each book individually, rifling through the pages, seeing if any slips of paper would fall out, words scribbled on a page, some kind of clue that would indicate where she was going.

They each went through one shelf a piece, neither having much to show for it. It was on the second shelf from the bottom where they found it. Or more accurately, Nicole found it. Flipping through the pages of a two-hundred-page puzzle variety book, it was there in the middle. Nicole went past it, assuming she wouldn't see anything, then flipped back to it when she saw it.

"Hey, I got something," Nicole said, taking the papers out.

There were several of them there. Two brochures and a piece of paper with some scribbling on it. She stood up as she examined them, handing the brochures to her partner as she examined the writing.

"Puerto Rico," Bridge said, looking through the pamphlets. He then looked at his girlfriend. "What else you got?"

"I'm not sure. A bunch of letters and numbers. Times. Could be flight times."

Nicole handed the paper to Bridge, who handed her back the brochures as each looked at what the other had. Bridge looked at the numbers and times on the paper. They did indeed look like flight times. He got out his phone and called Happ.

"Hey, I was already on the phone with your girl-friend an hour ago. I'm working on it."

"No, it's not that," Bridge said. "Well, it is that. Related to that."

"Just stop spitting up at the mouth and tell me what you want."

"We're in Ragland's room right now..."

"Legally?"

"Yes, legally. Her room is in her employer's house, who is standing right here and let us in."

"Well, that still could be messy if she had a lawyer that..."

"Can you stop thinking about the legal implications and just listen to me?"

"Sure. I guess I could do that."

"We just found some brochures with Puerto Rico on them. Figure she might be going there. Also found a piece of paper with what looks like flight times."

"Yeah? And?"

"You think you could run it down for us?"

"What am I, your personal assistant? You do know I have my own cases to work on, right?"

"You know how many favors we've done for you over the years? Coming to us with cases that you knew what was going on, but you didn't have the authority to touch?"

"How often are you gonna bring those up? It's only been a few."

"A few I didn't have to take."

"All right, all right, what do you have? I'll look into it."

Bridge took a picture of the paper with his phone, then uploaded and sent it to his friend. "Took a picture. Should be coming your way now."

"OK, I'll take a look at it. I have a friend at DHS who should be able to get a look at the security footage from the airport as well."

"Can't you just hack into it from your end?"

Happ faked a laugh. "Generally speaking, we try to do things the easy way first. You know, work with people, above board, before we start cutting corners."

"Oh. Well, suit yourself."

"Not all of us are mavericks, you know."

"Who are you calling a maverick?"

"I'm just saying."

"You think you can put a rush on that?" Bridge asked.

"Now you're pushing it. You really think I'm gonna have this for you within twenty minutes?"

"No, but an hour or two would be nice."

"What does Nicole see in you?"

"A bright, attractive, charming person?"

"I'll do what I can," Happ said. "But I can't make any promises with regard to time. You get it when you get it."

"That's fine. As long as it's within the next hour or two."

"You're impossible."

Bridge smiled, taking it as a compliment. "So they tell me. Anyway, I'm gonna start looking into flights, and I really don't want to already be on one by the time you get back to me on this."

"Didn't the last time you went and visited someone without having all the facts teach you anything?"

"Such as when?"

"Uh, Brazil?"

"Well, uh, that, uh, wasn't a... loss."

"Oh no? What would you call it? You went off down there, half-cocked, not having all the facts, having no evidence, and from what I hear, broke into the man's house and almost got killed."

"But we then found out that he didn't do it. So we eliminated him from the suspect pool. See? It turned out to be worthwhile after all."

"You really are a piece of work."

"Oh, and if you can, can you find out the woman that's with McClendon? I haven't really been able to check yet," Bridge said.

"You're a peach, you know that?"

"Thanks, I owe you one."

"One?" Happ said. "I think you've catapulted into double digits now."

"Who's counting?"

"I am."

"Oh. Well, just do this favor for me and I'll owe you one, OK?"

Happ grunted, then hung up. Bridge had a big

smile on his face as he put the phone back in his pocket, always liking the banter he and the FBI agent shared.

"So what's the deal?" Nicole asked.

"He's gonna work on it."

"So what do you wanna do from here? Wait to see what Eric comes back with?"

Bridge shook his head. "No, I don't wanna wait that long. They've already got a head start on us. We need to close the gap. I think we should check flights to Puerto Rico and then get on one."

Nicole got on her phone and started checking the flight schedules as Bridge began talking with Drewiskie. Within a few minutes, she had all that they needed.

"There's a non-stop flight to San Juan leaving in about five hours. Ten-hour flight."

Bridge nodded. "That's a flight we need to be on."

Bridge and Nicole then quickly said goodbye to Drewiskie, letting him know what they were doing and planning, then rushed out of the house to get back to their hotel so they could pack their bags again.

"What if we get to Puerto Rico and find out they're not there after all?"

"They're there," Bridge replied, getting behind the wheel of the car. "They're there."

"You're positive of that? Maybe those brochures were just research. Maybe they decided on somewhere else. Ever think of that?"

Bridge actually hadn't thought of that. He just immediately jumped to the conclusion that the brochures meant that was the destination they had chosen.

"Of course I have. I'm just sure that they're going to Puerto Rico."

"And if you're wrong?" Nicole asked.

"How often am I wrong?"

"The flight leaves in five hours. We don't have that much time for me to go into it."

"Ha ha, very amusing."

"I hope you're right about this and not just jumping to the wrong conclusion."

"Believe me, I'm right." Bridge then looked out the window, hoping that he was right.

It would not have been good if they actually got on the flight to Puerto Rico, then heard back from Happ saying that Ragland and McClendon actually boarded a flight to somewhere else. It would have been extremely embarrassing to eat crow on that one. It'd be another instance that Nicole would endlessly rib him on. And Happ as well. They seemed to take delight in mentioning times when he screwed up.

"Besides, the flight leaves in five hours, right?" Bridge said.

"Yeah."

"That gives Happy five hours to get the information we need. He'll come through. That's plenty of time."

"You saying that because you actually believe it or that if you say it enough times it'll actually be true?"

Bridge swallowed, a lump going down his throat. "Both probably. They've gotta be there. They've gotta be there."

19

Bridge and Nicole were waiting at the airport, an hour before their flight was supposed to leave. They were both anxious, hoping they weren't jumping to conclusions and making a mistake in thinking Ragland and McClendon were now in Puerto Rico. When Bridge's phone rang, he saw it was Happ, and immediately looked at Nicole as if he were afraid of what his friend might tell them. But at least if he got told that their targets weren't where they thought they were, at least they wouldn't have wasted their time flying there.

"Cutting it close there, buddy."

"Hey, these things take time," Happ said. "You know that."

"What do you got?"

"First off, it looks like you're right. They are in Puerto Rico."

As soon as he heard the words, he gave Nicole a

thumbs-up sign to let her know they were on the right track. "How do you know?"

"We got them on security cameras at the airport. Ragland, McClendon, and the girlfriend were all seen boarding a flight that we tracked to San Juan."

"When? How long ago?"

"Yesterday."

"We're not too far behind then."

"No, you're not. I've got something on the girlfriend too."

"What's that?"

"Her name is Jessica Lopez. Twenty-nine years old, been arrested two times before, minor stuff, nothing crazy."

"How do they tie in with Ragland?" Bridge asked.

"I don't know, that's a story for another day."

"Why Puerto Rico? Any ideas?"

"Well, you don't need a passport to go there for one since it's a U.S. territory. And maybe since two of them have criminal records, they thought they wouldn't be able to get one if they tried. Or maybe this trip was a last-minute thing, and they didn't have time to wait to get a passport."

"All possible."

"There's also one other thing."

"Which is?"

"I checked with a few guys who handle this sort of thing, know more than I do..."

"Wouldn't that be everybody?" Bridge asked, keeping his laughter in check.

"Couldn't resist, could you?"

"I really couldn't."

"Anyway, a few people I've talked to said they might be looking for a guy named Wilson Barajas."

"Who's that?"

"Apparently Barajas is a big player in the international market, buying, trading, fencing, all kinds of jewelry, including diamonds. The guys I talked to said if they're going to Puerto Rico, there's a good chance they'll be seeing him."

"You have anything else on him? Location?"

"Don't have a residential address for him, but we have some places that he likes to hang out. I'll email you a file so you can check it out on the plane."

"Thanks. Really appreciate you coming through like this, Eric."

"Hey, what are elite FBI agents for?"

Bridge smiled, unable to resist another chance. "I dunno, when I find one, I'll have him give you a call."

"Unbelievable."

Bridge finally let out a laugh. "Thanks."

"Don't get killed down there."

"I'll do my best."

Once off the phone, Bridge immediately relayed all the information to Nicole.

"That would make sense then," she said. "Barajas is the guy we gotta find."

"Those guys aren't always easy to find though."

"Sure they are. Once we find out the places he likes to go, we just go there, start making it known, well-known, I mean, loudly known, that we have some jewelry we want to get rid of. The people at those places obviously know him, know what he does, so it'll get back to him that we need someone. Then he'll magically appear."

"Question is, how much time will it take for that to happen?" Nicole raised her eyebrows. "And what happens if we can't find him before Ragland and McClendon sell those diamonds? Then it's like we're just chasing our tails. Because if we can't find them before they get sold, then we gotta track down who bought them, and it goes on and on."

"I don't think we have to worry."

"Oh yeah? Why not?"

"They just got on the plane yesterday. They're not that far ahead of us."

"What if they've already been in contact with Barajas? What if they've been setting this up for weeks? Then the score's already been settled."

Nicole raised part of her lip like something didn't agree with her. She knew Bridge was right, though. If everything was set up ahead of time, and an agreement was already in place, then there was a good chance they wouldn't get there in time before the sale went through.

The hour went by quickly, and as soon as they

boarded the plane, they opened the email that Happ had sent them. The FBI agent duplicated the email, sending it to both of them. It was a ten-hour flight that they both wished they could've sped up somehow, and while most people on the plane started to fall asleep, neither of them slept more than three hours. Once they had read the files several times, they came up with a plan, talking it over, changing it, until they finally came up with something that would work. Or so they hoped.

Once the plane finally landed in San Juan, they grabbed a separate rental car to go their own way.

"I still don't like splitting up," Nicole said.

"It's the only way we can make up some time. They've got twenty-four hours on us. We need to cut that in half. The best way to do that is by splitting up and knocking things off the list. If we do it together, it just takes longer."

Nicole then kissed him on the lips. "Stay out of trouble."

"Me? What about you?"

"Code word if one of us gets in trouble and we're actually able to contact the other?"

"Probably something simple, easy to say or type. How about... apple?"

"OK."

"Make sure we keep in touch with each other."

They got into their cars and drove off. They didn't even bother going to a hotel first to unpack. There was too much to accomplish first. There was a list of twelve places that Barajas was known to frequent, some more than others. Several were restaurants, two bars, a nightclub, a dry cleaner, a gas station, two tobacco shops, and a couple addresses that the business wasn't immediately clear.

First up on Bridge's list was a small restaurant, which couldn't have had more than twenty tables in the whole building. It looked like a small operation. Probably why Barajas liked it. Easy to keep tabs on everything and know what was going on versus a bigger business where things were constantly changing. If something was new, different, or out of place, he would know it.

In any case, Bridge sat down at a table near the front window and was greeted by a waiter. Though he really wasn't hungry, Bridge ordered anyway, just to give the appearance there was nothing unusual about him being there. He ordered a small sandwich, which he probably wouldn't finish, and a drink. As he waited for his food, Bridge looked around, seeing only three other tables occupied. About ten minutes later, his food came. Before digging in, Bridge started laying the seeds for a possible Barajas meeting.

"Hey, can I ask you something?"

"Sure," the waiter replied.

Bridge motioned for the waiter to move in closer, which he did. Bridge then looked around to make sure no one was listening, which made the waiter wonder what was going on. Bridge then started whispering.

"Hey, I got a problem, wonder if you could help."

"Possibly."

"You promise you won't say anything to cops or anything?"

The waiter shrugged, not sure what to say. "I guess."

"You know this town pretty well, huh?"

"I would say so."

"You happen to know anywhere I could get rid of a bunch of jewelry I got?"

"Stolen?"

Bridge let out an uncomfortable laugh. "See, this is what happened. I just got divorced. And my old lady took me for everything I had. I mean, everything. House, money, cars, the works. But I still found a way to stick it to her, you know what I mean?"

The waiter shook his head. "No."

"See, after the divorce went through, I went back into our house, the house that I paid for with my own money that she's now living in, the witch, and some of her jewelry just happened to fall in my pocket, you know what I'm saying?"

The waiter then nodded. "Ahh, I think I do."

"Yeah, so now I got a bunch of this stuff in my possession, and I wanna get it off my hands and put some money back into my bank account, know what I mean? An account she doesn't know about, you follow?"

"I believe I do."

"So you know anybody who's interested in this type of stuff? I mean, I'd obviously have to sell at a discount, I know that. But we're talking a few hundred thousand dollars of this stuff."

"Ahh, big bucks."

"Exactly. Do you know anybody who might be willing to take this stuff off my hands?"

The waiter immediately replied without much thought. "No."

Bridge's face looked surprised. He wasn't really expecting a name right off the bat, but he thought he'd at least get an "I'll think about it" or "I'll get back to you" or "I'm not sure", but no, he got none of that.

"Oh. OK. Well, do you know any other places around here that I might be able to check?"

"No."

The waiter then left, going into the kitchen area, out of Bridge's view. Bridge sighed, hoping the rest of the list wouldn't go as roughly as this did. Or else they were going to have a long night. He hoped Nicole was having a better go of it than he was.

Up first on Nicole's list was a tobacco shop. She walked in, looked around the place, then went up to the counter. There were two people in line ahead of her, so she patiently waited her turn. Once she got up there, she saw a disinterested-looking man behind the register, probably in his mid-thirties.

"Help ya?"

"Pack of smokes," Nicole said.

"Brand?"

"Whatever's cheapest. I'm on a budget right now."

The employee, still with a frown on his face, reached underneath the counter and forcefully put the cigarettes on the counter. Nicole then gave him the money for the merchandise, stuffing them into her pocket.

"Hey, can I ask you a question?"

The clerk shrugged, not looking very interested. "I guess."

"You know anyone who buys jewelry? Like, expensive jewelry? Because, like I said, I'm on a really tight budget, and as much as I don't want to, I gotta start selling some of my stuff. I've had some ex-boyfriends who've given me some really expensive stuff, like rings, necklaces, bracelets, things like that. I mean, the stuff's gotta be close to fifty thousand dollars."

"You got fifty thousand worth of jewelry you wanna get rid of?"

"Well, yeah, I guess. I mean, I'm not with them anymore, and I don't like looking at them and having them remind me of those clowns, and I've only got like two hundred dollars in my bank account, so, I need to do something."

The clerk shook his head. "Women. You got fifty

thousand dollars worth of jewelry just for looking pretty, and here I am slaving away in this joint, passing out tobacco for people who wanna kill themselves with cancer in a few years."

Nicole scrunched her eyebrows together, unsure of how to respond. "Uh, yeah, so, anyway, you know someone who buys this type of stuff?"

"Nope. Sorry."

"You don't know anyone?"

"Listen, lady, this is a tobacco shop. Not a pawn shop. You wanna sell some stuff, go there."

"But they'll try to rip me off."

"Probably."

"Look, I just want someone who will give me a fair price for them."

"And I'm not the neighborhood info man. Tell you what I'll do, you bring your stuff in, I'll look at it, and if I'm interested, I'll trade you a few cartons for it."

"A few cartons? For all my stuff?"

"You asked."

"I need money, not cigarettes," Nicole replied.

"And yet you're here."

Nicole grunted, then stormed off, not wanting to push the issue. She got in her car and checked the next place on her list. She hoped the next few places she visited would go a little better. But they weren't better. The conversation didn't go any better at the next few places she went. Some were lively, some were not, but the result was all the same. She used pretty much the

MIKE RYAN

same story, only changing it slightly from place to place, but nobody seemed to buy it. Either that or Barajas trained them all to be very careful about who they picked out to take to him.

The last place on Nicole's list for the day was a nightclub. She knew Bridge gave it to her specifically because he didn't want to go there. He would never admit such a thing, but she knew it to be true. The club opened at five, though she got there much later than that. It was already pretty busy when she arrived. She walked in, figuring she looked out of place considering she wasn't really dressed for it. She went to the bar and ordered a drink as she sized the place up, looking at all the patrons to see if anyone stood out to her. Though she hoped Barajas would miraculously show up, she wasn't counting on it. Instead, she made small talk with the bartender, flirting a little bit to try to extract some information. After a couple hours of not feeling like she was accomplishing much, Nicole figured it was time to meet Bridge back at the hotel, since he was already there waiting for her. But not before she made it well known that she had some jewelry she was looking to get rid of. She finished her drink, then headed for the door. Before getting there, she felt someone grab her arm, spinning her around.

"Hey, hey, where you going pretty lady?" the man asked.

"Away from you."

The man was joined by his two friends, one on

each side of him. They all started laughing. Judging by their mannerisms, the way they smelled, and the fact they couldn't seem to stand still, it was obvious they had way too much to drink.

"Don't go away so soon, come dance with us," the man said, moving in closer to her, attempting to touch her arm again.

Nicole was having none of that and easily pushed the man away. "I'd sooner dance with a rattlesnake."

The men laughed again. "Oh, come on now. Maybe if you don't feel like dancing, maybe we can just go back to my place and..."

Nicole wasn't about to let him finish his sentence. "Believe me, the three of you combined couldn't handle me."

"Whoa. So what you're saying is you want all three of us at once? I'd be OK with that."

"Eww. You're gross. First of all, I already have a boyfriend. Second of all, even if I didn't, I'd rather play with myself than touch you."

The men continued laughing, obviously blitzed out of their minds. There probably wasn't a thing Nicole could say that they wouldn't find amusing. The man's friends then motioned to him and then started moving to both sides of Nicole. She looked at them out of the corner of her eye, getting ready to put a hurting on them if they tried something.

"We done here?" Nicole asked. "Go back and play with the little girls that you're so used to having, because the big girls have real men waiting for them."

"I think I wanna play with you."

"Not gonna happen," she said.

Nicole then turned around, having enough of the conversation. She wasn't going to give them any more attention. As she started to leave, both men on her side grabbed each of her arms to prevent her from going. She didn't attempt to break free of them. She didn't have to. With her arms still being held, Nicole twisted her body to the left, kicking the man in the shin. After he dropped to a knee, he released his grasp of her arm, freeing her to spin around to deal with the other man. She then grabbed hold of the man's wrist and flipped him over, him landing hard on his back. Turning her attention back to the first man on the ground, she kicked him square in the face, sending him to the ground as well. A crowd of people had developed around the confrontation, not that Nicole had noticed. The second man that she flipped over was attempting to get back to his feet, though she quickly put a stop to that, giving him a back kick to the face that put him completely out of commission.

With the two friends down, Nicole then looked at the leader of the pack, walking slowly towards him. The crowd in the background started hollering, cheering her on.

"Kick his ass!" somebody yelled.

"Beat him down!" another shouted.

"Don't mess with her!" another said.

The man tried to back up, but the crowd kept him from completely getting away. Nicole stood directly in front of him, no more than a foot or two away, intimidating the man in the biggest way possible.

"Please, we were just having some fun."

"Fun?" Nicole said. "Fun? You think that's funny?"

"We were just trying to have a good time, that's all."

"You think trying to corner a woman is fun? You think putting your hands on one when she clearly isn't interested is fun? Do you understand how scary that could be for some women, having men crowd around her, afraid of what they might do?"

"Look, I won't do something like that again."

"I know you won't. You wanna know how?"

"Uh... how?"

"Because it's hard to do anything with your junk when it's in a sling."

The man looked confused, unsure of what she was saying. Nicole then looked at his legs, noticing that she had plenty of room to deliver a karate kick to the man's privates. The man immediately dropped to the floor in agony, holding himself. Her actions drew another loud cheer from the crowd that seemed to be enjoying her performance. For the first time, Nicole actually noticed them, and looked around at the faces. Once she saw they were on her side, she smiled at them. She figured it was time to leave, but before she left, she had another idea to teach the three a lesson. She went into their pockets, removed their wallets, and checked inside all of them. Collectively, the trio had about three hundred dollars in their possession. Nicole held it all up in the air for everyone to see, then walked over to the bar and handed it to the bartender.

"Looks like those three are buying drinks for the house!" Nicole shouted.

She immediately got another loud cheer, everyone going to the bar for their free drink. Nicole walked past them on her way to the door again, smiling at some of the customers' faces and actions, giving some of them high-fives as she exited the building. Just as she left, her phone rang.

"Hey, you all right?" Bridge asked.

"Yeah, I'm good."

"Sure are taking your time getting back here. Thought you'd be here by now."

"Oh, I, uh, had a little situation."

"Anything I need to worry about?"

"Nope. All taken care of."

"Need me to come down there?"

"I'm good."

"What happened?"

"You know, just the usual."

"Anything bad?"

Nicole looked back at the club and smiled. "Nothing I couldn't handle."

20

The following morning, Bridge and Nicole woke up, had breakfast in their hotel room, and discussed their plans for the day.

"You don't think we should hit up those places again?" Nicole asked. "Maybe swap lists?"

"Yeah, I don't think that would be a good idea. Makes us sound too desperate."

"We are."

"Also makes us seem too pushy. Like maybe we know more than we're supposed to. I think it would have the opposite effect and scare him off."

"Maybe."

"We made our play," Bridge said. "Hit all the places. Now we just have to hope it works."

"Or find Ragland and McClendon without him."

"Or that. Anything on your search?"

Nicole turned back to her computer. "No. I was able to get into the databases for the rental cars. Nothing that matched up with either of their names, or Lopez' either for that matter."

"Hotels? Airport footage?"

"Checked all the usual places. Still nothing. I can't find any trace of them anywhere."

"Which means maybe they got picked up by someone down here," Bridge said. "Maybe they got another partner who's local."

"Could be. Maybe it's Barajas."

Bridge nodded. "Could be."

While Nicole kept searching on the computer, Bridge was going to go out, without having a clear destination in mind. He was just going to go wherever, hoping inspiration would strike him when he got there. Or maybe he would visit one or two places they visited yesterday. In spite of what he'd told Nicole, they really had nothing else. Bridge gave his girlfriend a kiss and headed for the door when the hotel room phone began ringing. Bridge and Nicole looked at each other, then he calmly walked over and picked it up. He gave the usual greeting but didn't get one in return.

"Are you Mr. Bridgerton?"

"Depends who's asking."

"I believe you have been asking about me. My name is Wilson Barajas."

Bridge wasn't ready to give anything away. "Who?"

Barajas laughed. "Are we really going to play games here?"

"Not sure I know what you're talking about? Wilson was it?"

"You walked into several establishments yesterday, casually dropping hints about selling several large pieces of jewelry, did you not?"

"Oh, that! Were they your places?"

"Well, I do not own them. But I have friends who let me know of your interest."

"Who exactly are you? A buyer?"

"I might perhaps be interested if it's a large enough collection."

"We're talking over six figures."

"Impressive."

"What kind of payout are you looking for?"

"Well, how about you see the collection, then give me a fair offer and we'll see where we stand?"

"Sounds agreeable to me."

"Where would you like to meet?" Bridge asked.

"Let's make it that small restaurant, the one you ate lunch at yesterday. You remember it?"

"I do."

"Can you make it in three hours?"

Bridge looked at his watch. "I'll be there."

"Very good. I will see you there."

Bridge hung up, then stood there, like his shoes were frozen to the floor. He stared at the wall, contemplating what just happened.

"What was that?" Nicole asked.

Bridge looked at her, knowing she said something, though he didn't really hear it. "Hmm?"

"Who was that?"

"Oh, just Barajas."

"What?!"

"He just called. Heard I was asking about him. Well, the jewelry anyway."

"You wanna slow this up a little?"

Bridge replayed the conversation.

"You can't be serious about this," Nicole said.

"Why not?"

"It's obviously a setup."

"Think so?"

"Duh! Someone you talked to obviously got the jitters, maybe called Barajas, had you tailed from there. I'm sure he's done some digging on you since he was told you were asking about him. He just calls you up out of the blue at your hotel room? That's not normal."

"Didn't say it was."

"He knows you have no jewelry to sell."

"Probably."

"He's probably planning on killing you."

"I would think so."

"He knows you're not legit."

"Undoubtedly."

"But you're still gonna go."

"You got it."

Nicole slapped her head, then ran her fingers through her hair. "How do you think this is going to end up?"

"Probably like you said. He's gonna try to kill me."

"Aaannd? You're OK with that?"

Bridge shrugged, not seeing a problem with it. "I'm OK with him trying. I'd be upset if he succeeded."

"Luke, this is all kinds of bad."

"This is what we needed."

"How do you figure that?"

"We don't know where Ragland or McClendon are, right?"

"Right."

"We think Barajas might know, right?"

"Right?"

"So it stands to reason that if we talk to Barajas, he might tell us. Right?"

"Wrong."

"What?"

"He's not gonna tell us jack," Nicole answered. "He's probably going to have six guards with him, and he's probably going to shoot you on sight. Can't talk and ask questions if you're dead."

"He won't kill me on sight."

"You think not?"

"No," Bridge replied confidently.

"Why not?"

"Because he's going to want to find out if anyone

else knows about him, if I've told anyone else, if this is some kind of setup, if the authorities are closing in on him. There are a whole host of questions he's gonna want answers to."

"Or he could just shoot you and be done with it."

"Uh… maybe. Besides, that's what you're for. My protection. Right?"

"Why do I always have to rescue you out of some dangerous situation that you intentionally put yourself into?"

"Because that's how the job gets done."

"I really wish you'd think of some alternative ways to get things done."

"This way's more exciting."

"If you say so."

"Relax. It'll be fine."

"And just how am I supposed to protect you here?" Nicole asked.

"Well, I'll sit in the same booth I did yesterday. It was against the front window. There was a small hardware store across the street. You'll set up on the rooftop. If Barajas sits across from me, you should have a clear shot from the roof there."

"And how will I know whether to take the shot?"

"There was a napkin holder on the table. If I put my hand on top of it and leave it there, you take him out."

"And if you don't?"

"Then you let it ride. No matter what else happens, no matter what else you see, you let it happen."

"Even if I see them with a gun to your head?"

"If it looks like they have the advantage on me, it's because I want it that way for some reason. Just trust me on it."

Nicole sighed, not liking it, but willing to go along. "Fine. But what do you think he's going to do when he sees you have no jewelry to sell?"

"It's like you said. He knows that already."

"What if he's carrying a gun and just shoots you himself under the table?"

"He wouldn't do it there."

"He wouldn't?"

"No."

Nicole wondered how he could be so confident. "OK. Enlighten me."

"Well, he's not going to blow someone away inside one of the places he's known to frequent. Right there in broad daylight. Right?"

"I don't know. Won't he?"

Bridge shook his head, sure of himself. "He won't."

"I wish I had your level of confidence in someone we don't know even a little bit."

"Trust me. Guys like him, when they gotta kill someone, they'll do it in private. They only kill people in public when they wanna make an example out of someone. I haven't made him mad enough for that yet."

"Maybe you should have become a shrink. You seem to think you analyze everyone correctly."

"Nah. Way too boring."

"What are you hoping will happen here? Best-case scenario."

"We have a productive conversation, and he tells me where Ragland and McClendon are."

"You're living in a fantasy world if you think that's going to happen."

"Well, you asked for the best-case scenario," Bridge said. "Not the most likely scenario."

"Which would be?"

"Most likely? He takes me somewhere remote with the intention of killing me."

"And that's preferable why?"

"Because at some point, probably between us sitting at the table, and wherever he decides to take me, he'll tell me if he knows anything about our targets or the diamonds or both. And then wherever he takes me, you'll swoop in and save the day."

"Oh, just like that. Sounds so easy."

"Well, it's not complicated."

"And why do you think he would tell you anything?"

"Because people have a tendency to flap their gums and reveal anything when they think you won't live long enough to repeat it to anyone else. It's like some kind of human condition or something. They just can't help themselves."

"Dr. Bridge again speaking?"

Bridge shrugged. "Just something I've picked up over the years."

Nicole still had a bad feeling about all this, despite her boyfriend's confidence. "I hope you know what you're doing."

"So do I."

21

Bridge was sitting at the table, looking out the window, waiting for his guest to arrive. He and Nicole had arrived at the restaurant thirty minutes prior to that, making sure that they got there first. Bridge hated being second to a party of two. Then Bridge saw a couple of black cars pull up, newer-looking, tinted windows, waxed and shined. Bridge looked at his watch. One minute before the meeting time. He watched four men exit the vehicles, one of which was Barajas. He walked into the restaurant, one of his guards with him, while the other two stayed outside by the door. As soon as Barajas entered the restaurant, he and Bridge locked eyes, keeping them fixed on each other as the man walked over to the table.

"Mr. Bridgerton?"

"Mr. Barajas." Bridge put his hand out toward the empty seat. "Please. Have a seat."

Barajas unbuttoned his suit jacket as he sat down. "So, about this merchandise you have?"

Bridge grinned, appreciating the man was still sticking with the story. "I think we can both drop the charade now."

"Charade?"

"I don't have any jewelry to sell, you know that, and I know that you know. So let's both just drop the act and get down to what I'm really here for."

"Which is?"

"The truth is, I'm looking for a couple people who I think may have contacted you recently."

"And? Who are you? FBI, CIA, DEA, what?"

"I'm none of those things. Not anymore. I used to work for the CIA, but that was before. I work for me now."

"Doing what? What does any of this have to do with me?"

"I already told you," Bridge said. "I'm tracking down a couple of people who stole some diamonds. The owner wants it back."

"And you think I have them?"

"We're talking millions of dollars worth of diamonds. I've been told if they wanted to sell them, they'd be talking to you."

"What makes you think these people are even here?"

"We tracked them to a plane from Los Angeles to

San Juan. We know they're here. If they have contacted you yet, they soon will."

"And what do you think I can do for you?"

"I want the diamonds and I want them."

"And you believe I will hand them over to you? Why would I do that?"

"Because I have friends in the FBI, I used to work for the CIA, I even have contacts in the DEA. I could make life very difficult for you if I put the word out to have people look into you more closely."

"Threats are not something I take lightly, my friend."

"I'm not trying to threaten. All I want is those diamonds, and the people responsible for taking them, and then I'm gone. Nothing ever has to get back to you."

"Suppose I have the diamonds. Money has already been exchanged."

"We can get the money back for you. They haven't had time to spend it."

Barajas looked out the window for a moment. "This would set up a dangerous precedent for me. If what you say is true, any of it, and I give the diamonds back, or even if I don't have them yet and renege on my deal, that makes me look very bad. My reputation takes a hit."

"No one will know outside of us and the people who will be going to jail. And they won't be talking much."

"And what do I get out of this? Sounds like I'm doing you a favor but getting nothing in return."

"You're not a dumb man, Mr. Barajas. I think you know what extra heat down here would mean for your business."

"You would just turn a blind eye toward that?"

"I don't give a snowball in July about what you're doing down here. Doesn't concern me. All I want is what I've expressed to you."

"I will have to think on it."

"This is an instant offer," Bridge said. "It expires in about ten minutes."

"What happens then?"

"It gets a lot hotter."

"I see. Well, you don't give me much of a choice then, do you?"

"Not so much."

Barajas got up and adjusted his suit. "We should go then."

"Where are we going?"

"You want the diamonds, do you not?"

"I do."

"And you want the people who took them, no?"

"I do."

"Then you should come with me."

Bridge got up, and as he did, Barajas' guard came over to him and frisked him. He took a gun from Bridge's belt, who offered no resistance upon losing it. Bridge knew the deal. Men like Barajas didn't do business with people who were armed. Not if he could help it. And Bridge knew he wasn't going anywhere if he was. With Nicole looking over his shoulder, he felt he was still adequately protected anyway.

The three men walked out of the restaurant, then walked over to one of the cars, Bridge being placed in the back seat of the car that belonged to Barajas. His host sat next to him. Once they started moving, a hood was placed over Bridge's face, though his hands remained free.

"This is simply to keep you from knowing the location we are bringing you to," Barajas said. "Please do not remove it or we will make other arrangements."

"I'm sure those aren't as nice," Bridge replied.

"They are not."

Hoods had been placed over Bridge's head so many times it didn't even bother him anymore. If Barajas only knew how many times Bridge had to deal with that in his CIA training, he wouldn't have even bothered. It wasn't even a long drive, at least not in Bridge's mind. He was prepared for an hour or two of having the dark hood over his face. He was pleasantly surprised when the car stopped after half an hour. The men got out of the car, Bridge's hood was pulled off his face, then he was removed from the vehicle. Bridge looked at the building that was in front of him. It looked like some car repair shop. Or at least it used to be. He didn't see any cars anywhere on the outside.

Two of Barajas' guards got behind Bridge and gave him a little shove to move forward, which he did. They all went inside the building, which did have a couple cars inside the bays, looking like they were being worked on.

"Oh, this really is a car repair shop," Bridge said with a laugh.

"What did you expect?" Barajas asked.

"An abandoned building. So many of you guys choose abandoned buildings to work out of. I mean, I get it, it's easier to do things without any eyes watching, but this is a refreshing change. Doing business in an actual business." Bridge clapped his hands. "I applaud you for not stooping down to the stereotype."

Barajas didn't seem enthused, not even breaking a smile. "The diamonds are this way."

The guards pushed Bridge along to follow their boss, going towards a door that he guessed led into an office. He was right. What Bridge didn't count on was seeing a few familiar faces already sitting in there once he walked in. Ragland he knew on sight. But the pictures of McClendon and Lopez were spot on with their real appearance.

"I believe these are the people that you seek?" Barajas asked.

"That they are."

"This presents me with a bit of a problem."

"No problem from where I stand," Bridge said. "Just

give me my gun back, and I'll take these three into my custody and we'll be out of here."

"You see, the problem is that I've already made a deal with these people."

"Thought we already talked about that."

"But what we didn't talk about was money. See, they've agreed to sell me these diamonds for two million dollars. The diamonds are worth five. That means if I turn around and sell them tomorrow for three million, I've already made a million dollar profit. And if I wait a couple of years, the price will only go up. I can make an extra two, three, four million. That's a lot of money."

"Can't spend what you don't have. And you don't have anything if you're locked up or dead."

"I was thinking on the way over here about what you said. About having extra heat on me if I didn't do as you requested."

"That's right."

"And I thought to myself, what heat? If you're not around to tell anyone about this, there will be no heat. Am I right?"

"No. You're wrong. You're dead wrong. People know I'm here. They're gonna put two and two together and know what you did."

"I think not." Barajas motioned for the other three people to stand up. "I think I will not side with you on this matter."

"You're making a really big mistake," Bridge said.

"I think the only mistake I would make is allowing you to live."

Bridge smiled, then laughed, knowing what was coming next. "You don't wanna do that."

"I think the matter's been settled."

"Wait, he has a partner," Ragland said. "A girl."

"Yes, I know all about her," Barajas replied. "I was told she made quite the scene at a nightclub last night. Someone has been sent to their hotel room for her."

"OK, fine, kill me, but keep her out of it," Bridge said. "She's in the room, minding her own business, just put her on a plane and she won't be a problem."

"I have not yet determined the outcome for her. She may be someone I could use in my organization if she's willing."

"That's a mistake," Ragland said. "She's with him."

Barajas looked at the housekeeper. "That is a judgment I will make later. You have the diamonds with you?"

McClendon held a pouch up, confirming that they did.

"Excellent." Barajas looked back at Bridge. "Well, I don't think your presence is required here any longer."

"Well, let's..."

"Take him out back and do away with him."

The guards instantly took each of Bridge's arms, leading him out of the room. Bridge resisted, at least putting up the front that he was trying. He knew any attempt to escape would have to come outside, where the numbers were smaller. If he did it inside, there were too many people to successfully get away. But if there were only two outside, he figured he could handle that. Before they got to the back door, another guard joined the party, holding the door open for a clean exit from the building.

The four men, Bridge and the three guards, stepped outside, leaving the small patch of dirt that was around the building and walking towards a grassy area. As they walked, Bridge put his hand up and turned around to ask a question.

"What do you want?"

Bridge sighed, knowing he was going to have to make his move soon. He was just stalling for the right opportunity. He then saw a small red dot blink on one of the men's shirts. He then breathed a sigh of relief, knowing who was there with him. Now he just had to wait for her.

"You guys know what past dead means?"

The guards looked at each other, thinking he was crazy. "What?"

"Past dead. It's kind of like a phrase we used to use when I was in the government."

"What are you talking about?"

"Well, when you say someone's past dead, that means they've been marked for death, and their death is imminent, but they just don't know it yet. That's kind of like you guys."

"What did you just say?"

"I said you guys are past dead. You're basically dead. You just don't know it yet. But you will soon."

"Keep walking you—"

The man never got to finish his sentence, the bullet from Nicole's rifle lodging in the middle of his chest. The man next to him looked at his friend going down, then joined him two seconds later, a bullet finding him in almost the same spot as his buddy. The last guard raised his gun at Bridge, ready to fire, but Nicole was able to eliminate him before he could pull the trigger, the bullet going through his neck.

Bridge looked back, seeing his girlfriend's face next to a tree that she had been hiding behind. Bridge then reached down and took each of the pistols off the dead men. He raced back to the building, Nicole running to catch up to him.

"Thanks. I wasn't sure you had time to get in position yet."

"I literally got there just as they were bringing you out of the building," Nicole replied.

"Just the way we drew it up, right?"

"Uh, no. What happened?"

"Everything's in there. The diamonds, Ragland, McClendon, everyone. They're in the office now, doing the deal."

"How many guards?"

Bridge looked down at the ground, trying to remember, then looked back at the dead men. "Let's see, we took three out, one, two, three more there, should be five guards, plus Barajas, then our three suspects."

"Oh. Well, at least the odds are on our side."

Bridge placed his hand on the door handle, then flung the door open, leading the way inside. They both stayed low to the ground, heading for a car that was nearby. One of the guards saw them come in and started firing at them. Bridge and Nicole each hid behind the bumper of a separate car only a few feet away from each other. They rose up to return fire, hitting the guard at the same time.

"Pretty good teamwork there," Bridge said.

"I'm sure he appreciated it."

Hearing the gunfire, a few men came out of the office area. Bridge and Nicole each hit one of the men, dropping them both. Another of the guards came in through the front door, Nicole seeing him and hitting him with two shots. There was a brief lull in the action, with Bridge and Nicole wondering what the rest of them were doing.

"What do you think they're waiting for?" Nicole asked.

"I don't know."

They found out only a few seconds later. Barajas, his remaining guard, McClendon, and Lopez all fled out of the room at the same time, firing their weapons and running toward the front door. They were trying to make their getaway.

"There they go!" Bridge yelled, returning fire.

Nicole did the same as a massive barrage of bullets were fired in each direction. Lopez was the first to drop. The three men then got to the door and turned around to fire another shot to aid in their escape. Bridge nailed McClendon in the chest, as Nicole drilled the guard, both of them dropping to the ground. Barajas made it outside, Bridge running after him to cut off his escape. Barajas made it to his car and opened the door. Before he was able to get in, he saw Bridge by the door of the building and fired an errant shot that wasn't close to hitting his target. Bridge returned fire, not missing his target. The bullet found the middle of Barajas' forehead. Once he dropped to the ground, Bridge returned inside.

He saw Nicole bringing Ragland out of the office. She placed Ragland's back against the wall as she checked one of the nearby bodies, which was Lopez. Ragland stood there for a few moments, then looked down and saw Lopez' gun, which had fallen from her hand. She quickly reached down and grabbed the gun. Ragland pointed it at Nicole, who didn't make a move.

"Don't do that, Denise," Bridge yelled. His gun was aimed at her chest. Nicole spun her head around to see what was going on behind her, though she was careful not to move the rest of her body and cause the housekeeper to panic.

"I can't go to prison," Ragland said.

"It's better than being dead."

Ragland shook her head. "No, it's not."

She then swung her arms up, ready to fire on Bridge, who pulled the trigger one time. One time was all it took. He hit his target in the chest, killing her instantly. Nicole went over to her and checked her vitals. She stood up, shaking her head.

"Shouldn't have turned my back on her."

Bridge came over to Nicole and put his arm around her. "She didn't seem the type who would do something like that."

"There is no type."

"Yeah, I was just trying to make you feel good."

"You wanna know what will really make me feel good?"

Bridge laughed. "I can guess."

Nicole held the pouch of diamonds in her hand. "Our work is done here. Drewiskie will be happy."

"I would think so."

"Hey, what were you talking about with those guys outside before I took them out?"

"Oh, I was just telling them they were past dead."

"What? Did you really tell them about that stupid old saying? It doesn't even make sense."

Bridge smiled. "It doesn't have to make sense. Just has to keep them busy long enough for you to take them out. Which it did. See, it worked."

Nicole shook her head. "It's still dumb."

Bridge shrugged. "It just has to keep them occupied."

"I guess."

"Anyway, you're right, Drewiskie will be happy we got the diamonds back. We won this one."

"Great. Let's go back to the hotel so you can help me feel happy."

"I can go for that."

ABOUT THE AUTHOR

Mike Ryan is a USA Today Bestselling Author. He lives in Pennsylvania with his wife, and four children. He's the author of the bestselling Silencer Series, as well as many others. Visit his website at www.mikeryanbooks.com to find out more about his books, and sign up for his newsletter. You can also interact with Mike via Facebook, and Instagram.

 facebook.com/mikeryanauthor

instagram.com/mikeryanauthor

ALSO BY MIKE RYAN

Continue with the next book in The Extractor Series,
Pressure Point.

Other Books:

The Silencer Series

The Eliminator Series

The Cain Series

The Brandon Hall Series

The Ghost Series

A Dangerous Man

The Last Job

The Crew

Printed in Great Britain
by Amazon